FORTUNE BABY ON THE WAY!

It's a landmark day in Sioux Falls—Nash Fortune is going to be a first-time granddaddy! But apparently Nash is blowing a gasket over the fact that his grandbaby was conceived out of wedlock. (Turns out his virginal daughter, Skylar, got knocked up by a mysterious New Zealander during her brother's wedding!) Too bad Nash's third wife, Patricia, ran out on him—she had a knack for putting a positive spin on their disgraceful family scandals!

Hmmm…we have to wonder why the drop-dead gorgeous daddy-to-be is pressing so hard to get a ring on Skylar's finger and whisk her across the...

Our ...

whisper that Zack has a checkered past that rivals anyone in the Fortune clan. And history seems to be repeating itself for this charming bloke. Years ago, Zack was caught up in a messy situation with another pregnant girl who "coincidentally" also came from a wealthy family who liked to run roughshod over everyone.

If I were Skylar Fortune, I'd get myself an iron-tight prenup before waddling down the aisle!

D0830284

Dear Reader,

We're so glad you're back for more of the DAKOTA FORTUNES. This family has its share of drama and scandals. And what better scandal than a secret baby? Youngest daughter Skylar Fortune had a clandestine affair with a certain handsome New Zealander and now she's having his baby. But none of her siblings—or her overprotective father—have figured out the truth yet. So just imagine what's going to happen in Jan Colley's EXPECTING A FORTUNE.

And then next month—though it's hard to believe—we're wrapping up the six-book continuity with FORTUNE'S FORBIDDEN WOMAN by Heidi Betts. This much-anticipated love story will answer all your questions about the entire series…and give Creed the woman he's always desired.

Here's hoping you enjoy this fabulous story!

Best,

Melissa Jeglinski

Melissa Jeglinski
Senior Editor
Silhouette Desire

Please address questions and book requests to:
Silhouette Reader Service
U.S.: 3010 Walden Ave., P.O. Box 1325, Buffalo, NY 14269
Canadian: P.O. Box 609, Fort Erie, Ont. L2A 5X3

JAN COLLEY

EXPECTING
A FORTUNE

Silhouette®

Desire

Published by Silhouette Books
America's Publisher of Contemporary Romance

Thanks to Peter Mounce, brother-in-law and font of knowledge
on the thoroughbred horse-breeding industry; to Kelli Lowe,
a friend who conveniently participated in the same phase of pregnancy
as the heroine of this book and shared her "bump" stories with me
(Hello to beautiful baby boy Alex!) and to Debbie and Paul Thistoll
of the Emerald Lodge Stud near Christchurch, who gave up their precious time
to show me around their busy and successful stud farm.

Special thanks and acknowledgment are given to Jan Colley
for her contribution to the DAKOTA FORTUNES miniseries.

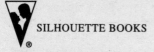 SILHOUETTE BOOKS

ISBN-13: 978-0-373-76795-3
ISBN-10:   0-373-76795-1

EXPECTING A FORTUNE

Books by Jan Colley

Silhouette Desire

Trophy Wives #1698
Melting the Icy Tycoon #1770
Expecting a Fortune #1795

JAN COLLEY

lives in Christchurch, New Zealand, with her long-suffering fireman and two cats who don't appear to suffer much at all. She started writing after selling a business because at tender middle-age, she is a firm believer in spending her time doing something she loves. Jan is a member of Romance Writers New Zealand and Romance Writers of Australia, and she is determined that this book will be one of many. She enjoys reading, traveling and watching rugby, and would be tickled pink to hear from readers. E-mail her at vagabond23@yahoo.com.

THE DAKOTA FORTUNES

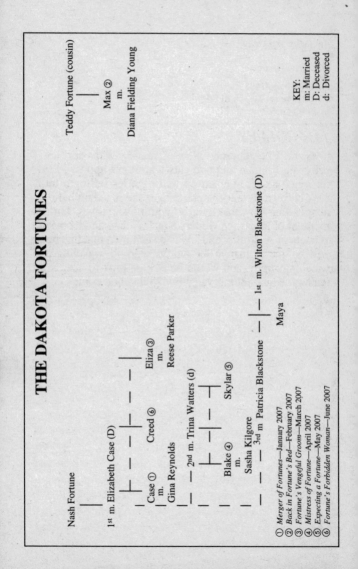

Teddy Fortune (cousin)

Max ②
m.
Diana Fielding Young

Nash Fortune

1st m. Elizabeth Case (D)

Case ①
m.
Gina Reynolds

Creed ⑥

Eliza ③
m.
Reese Parker

2nd m. Trina Watters (d)

Blake ④
m.
Sasha Kilgore

Skylar ⑤

3rd m. Patricia Blackstone

1st m. Wilton Blackstone (D)

Maya

① *Merger of Fortunes*—January 2007
② *Back in Fortune's Bed*—February 2007
③ *Fortune's Vengeful Groom*—March 2007
④ *Mistress of Fortune*—April 2007
⑤ *Expecting a Fortune*—May 2007
⑥ *Fortune's Forbidden Woman*—June 2007

KEY:
m: Married
D: Deceased
d: Divorced

One

Skylar pressed Send and waited for the personalized world clock to do its thing.

"Sioux Falls, South Dakota, U.S.A," she read off the screen. "Friday, 9:06 p.m. Christchurch, New Zealand, Saturday, 4:06 p.m."

Would he be working?

Scraping her fingernails along damp palms, she drew in a ragged breath and hopefully a bucket of courage. Too long had passed, about three months too long, but she could hide it no longer.

Phone, address book…her fingers raced around the desk, tidying the jar of pens, straightening papers. Should she make a drink or go to the bathroom first? *If you want to make an easy job seem mighty hard, just keep putting off doing it. Who said that?* she wondered, then a knock at the door cranked up her heartbeat. A welcome relief? A stay of execution? But the butterflies stayed with her as she rose, tugging her long shirt down over her sweats.

It was easy to avoid people, living in the cottage by the stables, away from the prying eyes of the main house on the estate. No one had noticed a thing, but that wasn't surprising. After all, who ever noticed Skylar? But the concern in her brother's eyes on a rare visit from Deadwood last week came back to her now.

"Coming." Skylar yanked the door open and nearly passed out on the spot.

Zack Manning opened his mouth then closed it again with an audible snap, or that might have been the sound of her knees buckling.

He stared at her, the beginnings of a smile on his handsome face fading fast.

Her worst nightmare. Adrenaline flooded her system and she could not look away. She felt her lips move in a soundless prayer, felt the tension in her fingers, balled into fists by her sides.

After an age, he lowered his gaze, straight to her midriff. Released momentarily, she sagged against the doorjamb, but her relief was short-lived. Incredulous gray eyes shot back to her face, pinning her again, and she watched his tanned face leach slowly of color.

Skylar swallowed. "Zack," she said, her tone just above a whisper. *Deny everything.* He couldn't see what she had hidden under her long checked flannel shirt.

"When did you think you might put me in the picture?"

Skylar's head dropped and she stared at her feet. "I was just— I just got off the Net. The world clock…" Her voice trailed off. Did she expect him to believe that when she was four months pregnant and hadn't bothered before now?

The crown of her downcast head prickled under his glare. Sighing, she moved to the side so he could enter. Skylar closed the door as he brushed past but did not turn immediately. Instead she leaned her forehead on the door, gathering her jumbled thoughts, but the truth of it was, she had no idea what to say.

Slowly she turned. Zack prowled the lounge of her cozy little cottage and he looked furious. Tightly controlled, but furious. His tall rangy form bristled with tension, his mouth was set in a harsh line.

She hovered by the door, hoping she didn't look as tragic as she felt.

Zack suddenly came to a halt and leaned forward with his large hands spread on the battered leather of her old sofa. "We used protection." His voice was flat.

Skylar's first thought was surprise that he did not question the baby's paternity, that he automatically assumed this was his child. Then she bit her lip to stop a rogue smile. Who would want her? After all, she'd been a virgin that night back at the beginning of February.

"The…it broke, I guess." She kept her face down, unable to even say the word. Her face felt hot enough to fry an egg on. How excruciating, to be discussing this with him. "I thought—" her breath hitched "—it might have, when Maya was here."

Her best friend had burst into the unlocked cottage almost the moment they'd finished. Skylar had panicked, vaulting from her bed, pushing at him while throwing a robe on. Maya had a habit of just walking up the stairs and into her bedroom.

"I think I would know!" His voice was low with an icy undertone.

Her shoulders jerked as she recalled the desperate whispers, how she had pushed him into her bathroom and closed the door. There was just enough time to kick his clothes under the bed and straighten the covers before a tearful Maya walked into the room.

Aside from the fantastic sex, it was a pretty lousy end to her first time.

"I would have known!" he insisted.

"The light was out," Skylar whispered. Images of herding him into her bathroom played through her mind like a film clip. His hand reaching for the light switch. Her hand slapping it away. "You probably couldn't see."

"And you didn't think to mention it at the time?"

"I wasn't sure." She rubbed her forehead, sighing wearily. It was her first time, how was she supposed to know? And even if she did, there was no way she could have broached such an intimate subject. Not with him. "I didn't—didn't think I knew you well enough."

"Didn't *know* me well enough?" He made a harsh sound that might have been a laugh.

"It wasn't like we were in a relationship," she mumbled. "It was just too embarrassing, talking about—stuff like that."

She flicked him a nervous glance and a ray of hope soothed her a little. His mouth was more relaxed. A wash of anger still mottled his cheeks but his brows creased more in confusion now. Maybe he believed her.

"I couldn't see a thing," he said, as if to himself. "I just disposed of it and waited for you to get Maya out of the bedroom." He glanced at her sharply. "You were pretty keen to get rid of me then."

Skylar walked over to the dining table and sat. "I thought I'd be spared—" she clasped her hands, prayer-like, on the table "—since it was my first time."

His tone was incredulous. "Skylar, you breed horses. Virgin or not, surely you understood the implications of unprotected sex."

Squeezing her hands together, she nodded miserably.

Zack leaned on the couch, his eyes boring into her. It was done. The worst was over. She cast him some furtive looks and his well-remembered features began to make an impact on her already heightened senses. Skin like his loved the sun and her own pale arms, bare from the elbow, looked insipid compared to his healthy tan. New Zealand's seasons were the opposite to here and South Dakota was just out of a long, cold winter. His sandy hair was still short at the back but longer than she remembered at the sides and front. The deep dimples that traced a line from his well-defined cheekbones to his strong chin were not in evidence tonight. Skylar had fallen head over heels for those dimples almost at first glance.

"Does anyone else know?"

She shook her head. Avoiding the family and her monthly nights out with Maya wasn't difficult when it was the busiest time of the year for the Fortune Stud.

"When were you thinking of telling them? After the birth, or…"

His sarcasm intensified her guilt. "I'm sorry."

"You're sorry." Zack began pacing the room again, as if he was circling his prey.

"I don't—hold you responsible or anything."

"What?" The tension in his quiet voice screamed through her nerves.

"I mean, financially…"

There was a long, excruciating silence.

She sighed, still not looking at him. "I mean, this doesn't have to encroach on…"

Zack sat down suddenly, as if all the air had just gone out of him. "No," he said dazedly, "I'm only the father."

He was ashen. Skylar rose, guilt clawing at her throat. "Do you want something? A drink?"

"Are you seeing someone?" He peered up at her in a lightning change of tack.

She ducked her head with a disbelieving smile, as if he'd said something ridiculous. "No." She twisted her hands together. "Who?"

His suspicious appraisal was unwarranted.

"What are you doing here, anyway? I thought you weren't coming back till the fall."

"Blake called," he muttered. "He was worried about you, said you weren't yourself."

"He shouldn't have done that."

"Done what?" he asked.

"Gotten you involved."

Zack bared his teeth mirthlessly. "Since I'm only the father."

"He doesn't know anything."

"Makes two of us!" he barked, and Skylar jumped. There was an indeterminate slide inside that she'd only felt a couple of times before, and her hand instinctively went to her stomach.

"What is it?" Zack leapt to his feet. "What's wrong?"

She looked up and blinked at the concern in his eyes. "Nothing."

"Why are you holding your stomach?"

"The baby moved."

The look on his face shocked her, as did the jerky movements of his big hands as they dragged through his sandy hair.

"I can't believe this," he grated, "You're—what? Four months pregnant, the baby's moving and I've only— I didn't know a thing."

That was pain darkening his eyes, she was sure. Pain making his voice sound raw.

"And I'm not to have any part of it?" Zack clipped out. "You want to cut me out of everything?"

Skylar twisted her hands together. "It's not like that." She shuffled on her feet, not knowing what to do or say to make things right, or if not right, better.

"I think I will have that drink," he told her curtly, after long moments had passed.

Why had she offered? The only alcohol Skylar had ever kept in the house was the odd bottle of wine if Maya was coming by. The day her pregnancy was confirmed, she'd thrown out a half-empty bottle in her fridge.

She peered at a dusty bottle of some apricot liqueur that must have been there for three or four years, then closed the cupboard and poured him a glass of water.

As soon as he'd taken it from her, she moved back, turning away from the waves of anger she sensed building in him again. She tottered a few steps, turning from him and heard his hard swallow.

What a mess. The word *sorry* danced around and around her mind, along with *clumsy, clueless, stupid.* The silence dragged on and she chewed on her thumbnail. "Where are you staying?"

Zack rapped out the name of Sioux Falls most prominent hotel, the Fortune's Seven, one of several her brothers owned.

Sleeping with him was the dumbest thing she'd ever done, although at the time, it surpassed all her amassed curiosity and fantasies. She should stick to horses for company. She'd never had a problem talking to horses. They didn't judge or reduce her to a quivering mass of nerves and resentment at her clumsy social skills.

"I'll take care of everything," she blurted, unable to take the silence anymore.

She heard another hard swallow. "That's great. That's just great, Skylar."

She spun around, stung by the bitterness in his voice. His searing eyes told her it was anything but great.

"The baby won't want for anything," she told him defensively. He must know that. She made good money doing what she was doing, quite apart from her heritage as one of the Fortune family. The city of Sioux Falls was practically owned by the Fortunes.

"Nothing but a father."

She sighed. "My father and Patricia will be crazy about a baby. And my brothers, well, they'll come around. The baby will be knee-deep in male role models."

"And you don't think that a biological father has any part in this warped family scene you've cooked up?"

"Zack, if you want to see it, have access, that's—that's okay."

"*Access?*" he snapped, prowling around her in an ever-decreasing circle.

Skylar flinched, blinking. "If you want. What *do* you want?"

He gave her a withering look. "Thanks for asking.

Pick a date. We'll get the whole family around tomorrow and tell them we're getting married."

"What?" It was her turn to be shocked.

"Make it quick, Skylar. I can't be away from home for long."

"Married?" she whispered, her head spinning.

He drained his glass and banged it down on the table. "My child is going to have two loving parents, not just one."

"I'm not marrying you, Zack." A hiccup escaped her throat. "Not marrying anyone."

He leaned down, his face inches from hers. "You may have cut me out of this till now, the worrying, the morning sickness, the movements. But that changes as of right now." She'd never seen his gray eyes glint like steel before. "We *are* going to be married, so get used to it."

She made a pitiful attempt at a smile. "That's just—dumb."

"What's dumb?" he demanded. "Pretending it hasn't happened? Hiding it from everyone? I suppose you could have delivered it in the stables and told everyone the stork left it."

His flippant remark stirred an unusual lick of anger. "Maybe this is why I didn't tell you. I was afraid you'd want to take over, have it all your way."

Her voice rang out, clear and strong, making them both start. Skylar seemed to have lost her stammer. Normally she was hard-pressed to string five words together around Zack Manning.

He recovered first. "You've had your way. It isn't good enough."

"I'm not marrying you, Zack."

"No kid of mine is going to be brought up without two parents and a wedding ring."

"This child will want for nothing," she repeated, stung at the assumption she couldn't provide for the baby.

This wasn't like her, to argue back. It must be her hormones kicking in. Her baby-protective hormones.

"No, it won't, because I'll take care of the both of you."

Incredulous, she just stared at him, shaking her head. "I don't believe you."

"Whatever." He shrugged and headed for the door.

"Where are you going?"

"If I'm not back in an hour, your father has used his shotgun on me."

"No!" Skylar leapt after him. "Zack, please. Let me tell him, my own way."

"You've had your way for four months. The next five are mine, I reckon."

She attempted to scoot around him to get to the door first. "He's an old man and he has problems of his own right now."

Zack blocked her with ease. "Your father is tough as an ox."

"Zack, Patricia has left him. He's devastated."

"Then a wedding to look forward to and a baby on the way should be just what he needs to take his mind off things."

"Will you please," she implored, "leave my father out of this until I've had a chance to think?"

Zack nearly combusted, his knuckles on the doorknob turning white. "A chance to think?"

"Just until I tell everyone. I'll keep you informed—"

He yanked the door open, rolling his eyes. "Yeah, right!"

Skylar was hot on his heels and having to run to keep up.

Zack turned on her. "Get back inside."

"I'm coming with you."

"Skylar, this is man's talk. You don't want to be there."

"Don't you patronize me!" Much as the note of panic in her voice disgusted her, she had to stall him.

"Calm down." He turned her, his hands surprisingly gentle on her shoulders and at odds with the harshness of his voice. "I'll be back soon."

"Dad's not at the house," she lied, desperate. "He had to go look for Patricia."

"Forgive me if I don't believe you."

"You're impossible!" she wailed.

"No, I'm a lamb." He propelled her back inside. "And you are a lying, conniving… Sit down." He settled her gently, insistently, into a chair. "And wait for me."

"When did I ever lie to you?" Skylar wondered if she could faint on cue. Any stupid female trick would do, just to keep him here.

He bent toward her, his face so close she felt his breath on her skin. "How about my twice-monthly phone calls, when I would ask how you were?" he suggested.

She bit her lip, her eyes wide. Trust him to bring that up.

"Did you not think to say, 'Fine, Zack. Pregnant. It's yours, but fine.'" He glared down at her then turned on his heel.

She slumped. It was true. She'd had ample opportunities to tell him he was going to be a father. How excited she'd been, the first time he called, yet embarrassed, too, at the less than perfect ending to their night of passion. In subsequent calls he'd suggested she come down to check out his new stud and also dropped hints about his return in September for the Keeneland Sales: "Maybe you could take a couple days off and come with me…" She was ever the blithering idiot, too shy to talk of anything other than horses.

Naturally, after she discovered she was pregnant, those conversations were torture and she wondered why he bothered. But to give him his due, he had always shown an interest, always asked after her.

A car engine started up outside, rousing her.

Her father! She had to warn him. Picking up the phone, Skylar quickly dialed the house and begged her father not to talk to him. "Get Peggy to say you're out," she demanded. Goodness knows she asked for little enough from her father.

Curious, Nash Fortune agreed, telling her to come up directly after Zack had gone.

A few minutes later, Zack returned, thwarted in his attempt to speak to her father. Grim and determined, he pushed his face close to hers. "If you are not here in the morning," he warned, "I will track you down. Count on it."

As soon as he left for town, Skylar drove up to the big house and her father opened the door. "What is going on, Skylar?"

He looked so tired. She hated having to dump this on him, after the day or so he'd endured. It wasn't a lie about her father's wife leaving him. "Any news on Patricia?"

Nash shook his head sadly. "No. What's Zack Manning got a bee in his bonnet about?"

"Sit down, Dad."

Two

Never again!

Zack swung the rental car out of the hotel parking lot and headed toward the Fortune Estate, about twenty miles west of the city of Sioux Falls.

Never again would he allow himself to be shafted by wealth and power. That was his domain now. He had more than enough to make Skylar's family squirm, should they play hardball.

His eye was drawn to the twenty-three-story Dakota Fortune building a block away, where Case and Creed, her half brothers, conducted their business. No doubt he'd have to deal with them at some stage, but his focus was on Nash Fortune this morning. Regardless of the man's marital upheaval, his daughter was four months' gone—four months!—and it was past time Nash knew what Zack's intentions were.

He rubbed his eyes, a sleepless night exacerbating a whole hemisphere of jet lag.

Focusing on what to say to Nash helped ease the burn of anger. Skylar clearly thought so little of him, she couldn't even tell him of the life they'd created. Sure, they barely knew each other, but he bristled at the notion that he was unapproachable where Skylar was concerned. He'd made a concerted effort to be pleasant to her on his visit here earlier in the year, especially when it became apparent how shy and uncomfortable being around him made her. Zack knew when someone was sweet on him.

His cell phone rang. It was Max Fortune, his closest friend and business partner in Australia and Skylar's cousin.

"What in blazes? You knocked up my little cuzzy, you bastard?"

Zack grinned. The Australian rancher was all bark and no bite where he was concerned. They'd been through a lot together.

Then he sobered. These big rich families moved quick. He hadn't said a word to anyone and already the southern hemisphere family grapevine was abuzz. "What do *you* want?" he drawled.

"To knock your block off, mate." There was a pause. "What are you going to do?"

Zack blew out a breath. "I'm on my way to see Nash now about making an honest woman of her."

There was a lengthy silence. The two men's self-imposed bachelorhood had come to a sticky end a few months ago when Max wed his old flame Diana. Zack imagined the sound of necks cracking as his friends and enemies did a double take at this second blow to confirmed bachelor status Down Under.

"What does Sky think about that?"

Zack had his own ideas about that. While tossing and turning in his hotel bed, he'd concluded that he'd walked into a setup the night of Case Fortune's wedding four months ago. Skylar's setup.

"She'll come around," he said shortly. "Who told you, anyway?"

"Nash called Dad. Gave us all a shock, that's for real. Dad told him, 'Don't trust that Kiwi, he's got sprogs all over the world and he's only out for your money.'"

Zack let out a bark of laughter and nearly missed his turnoff. "Tell the old reprobate thanks." He knew of Teddy Fortune's warm regard for him.

But there were some things the Australian Fortunes didn't know. Like the mistake eighteen years ago, when Zack had gotten his young sweetheart pregnant. Like the anger that had burned in his gut all these years, born of his helplessness as a penniless boy from the wrong side of the tracks who had been virtually run out of town. Helpless to stop Rhianne from giving in to her rich family's wishes to abort his baby and not ruin her life.

Never again…

"You'll, aah, you'll be nice, won't you, Zack? I like old Freckles, she's a good sort. I wouldn't have her hurt."

"I like her, too, Max," Zack reassured his friend quickly. "Wish me luck or I won't ask you to be best man."

He hung up, thinking with surprise that was true; he *did* like Skylar, more than he'd liked any woman in a long time. There was something about her right from the start, even though she did nothing to lead him on, until the night of that family wedding.

Shocked nearly senseless at the news he was going to be a father, there was not a shadow of a doubt in his mind that he and Skylar would marry. Even now, about to confront her father and cause this family all sorts of upset, there was only one course of action.

Love didn't come into it.

Just ahead, he saw the stone pillars that announced Fortune Estate land. Instead of turning off to Skylar's cottage in the stand of trees by the stables, he drove toward the big house, as she called it, thinking it was better Nash was prewarned, had had time to think about it.

Despite that, his stomach tightened as he approached the huge old mausoleum the Fortunes called home. A little too gothic for his taste; Zack preferred a more contemporary residence. The dark gray stone made it appear almost black and very forbidding. But inside, it was comfortable and homely, reflecting Patricia's warm personality.

He parked the car and took the steps leading up to the house two at a time. Peggy, the housekeeper, showed him into the dining room. Zack was surprised to find only Nash present. He'd expected one or two of the large family here at this time.

The older man looked up from his breakfast, his glum expression lightening. "Zack! Sit down. I hate to eat alone."

The two shook hands and Zack helped himself to juice and toast from the ample buffet and tried, unsuccessfully, to prevent Nash calling to Peggy to fix some fresh eggs.

"Where is everyone?" he asked, part of him disappointed he could not settle with the whole family in one sitting. They chatted for a couple of minutes about the whereabouts of the other residents of the house. Since Zack had left in early February, Nash's older daughter, Eliza, had moved to Montana to be with her husband, Reese. The other two sons, Case and Creed, divided their time between apartments in town and the estate.

Then Nash fixed him with a stern gaze. "So you're about to become a daddy."

"That's why I'm here."

"Congratulations." Nash's gaze narrowed as if trying to read his mind.

"Not sure that's appropriate, under the circumstances."

"New life is precious, whatever the circumstances." Nash finished his pancakes just as Peggy slid a plate full of freshly scrambled eggs in front of Zack. His mouth watered. He'd eaten nothing but plastic airline food in the last twenty-four hours.

"I like you, Zack," the older man continued. "You're a straight shooter. I believe your intentions are good."

"They are." Zack sent up a silent thanks to Teddy Fortune in Australia. "I asked her to marry me."

"Asked?"

Zack paused, a forkful of eggs on the way to his mouth. "More or less," he affirmed with a quick nod. "She won't have it."

Nash leaned back, his expression fond. "Skylar is a complicated girl," he said slowly. "It's hard to know what she's thinking. Her mother—well, she wasn't the mothering type."

Zack knew a little of the history. Skylar and Blake's real mother, Trina, was run off the Fortune Estate, sans children, when Nash discovered her cheating on him.

By all accounts, Patricia, Nash's third wife, was more of a mother to them than their own.

"I don't know Skylar as well as I should." Nash lifted his coffee cup. "She bottles things up. She's close to her brother, and Patricia and Maya, but doesn't seem to need the rest of us much." He gave a sad little smile. "We all think the world of her, but it's true, we're a family that doesn't talk easily about feelings."

"I'll take good care of her, sir. I know it'll be strange at first, a new country, being away from her family. But I'm in a position to give her anything she wants."

"What she wants? I think what she wants is her independence. And her horses. Girl always loved her darn horses."

"I have more than enough horses to keep her happy." Zack pushed his plate away and leaned his arms on the table. "It'll be a good life, Nash, and I'll bring her and the baby back whenever she wants."

"It's not me you have to convince." The older man sighed heavily. "There's too much goin' around in my old brain at the moment. Thing is, I don't think Skylar knows a lot about the ways of men. She's an innocent."

Not that much of an innocent, Zack thought grimly.

A flash of blue through the window caught his eye. Their subject mounted the steps outside. "Do I have your blessing, sir?" he asked quickly.

"My blessing?" Nash stuck his thumb in his belt, his tired blue eyes peering out under thick graying brows. "If you can get the girl to agree then…" He nodded slowly, then raised his head.

Skylar entered the room, looking mutinous. They both watched her approach and Nash inhaled sharply.

"How the heck did we all miss it?" he murmured. "It's as obvious as a poke in the eye she's expecting."

Both men stared at her candidly, though doubtless Zack's reaction was vastly different than her father's. To an outsider, she was dressed as normal: jeans, a longish flannel shirt with a shapeless navy jacket over the top. Her light brown hair shone in braids, what he could see of it, with her signature baseball cap jammed on top.

The moment she'd opened the door last night, the knowledge that she was pregnant hit him like a sledge-hammer between the eyes. *Wham! She's pregnant. Wham! It's mine.*

Wham! Not again...

He'd always considered her pretty. Her wide mouth turned up at the corners with a sweetly pronounced bow in the middle. Arched brows dipped low in the middle of her forehead in that interesting way some women had that looked like they were on the verge of frowning. The old adage about pregnant women glowing was true, the proof of it standing in front of him now. A luster to her creamy skin, freckles seemed more pronounced, her eyes more blue. In his mind, the shy and scruffy tomboy who never looked him right in the eye, had been replaced by one hellishly attractive woman.

One very ticked off woman. As if she could read his thoughts, she glared at him, her chin tilted up defiantly. "What are you doing here, upsetting my father?"

Nash raised his hand. "Now, now. He's not upsetting me. We're just having a chat."

She kept her eyes on Zack. "About me, naturally."

Zack folded his arms, torn between a worrying stab of desire and annoyance.

"Get yourself some breakfast, girl," her father ordered. "Let's talk this thing out."

Skylar narrowed her eyes even more for good measure then stalked to the buffet and poured some juice into a glass. She returned to the table and sat.

Zack looked pointedly at the glass. "Shouldn't you eat something?"

"Don't start," she retorted.

Both guns blazing, he thought with wonder. Where had this spitfire been hiding?

Nash looked at her daughter. "Zack has asked me for your hand."

She scowled. "How quaint. Is that a New Zealand custom?"

"Skylar," Nash hushed her. "Do you like him at all?"

She exhaled and looked away with a shrug.

"Well, I assume you liked him well enough to make a baby with him," Nash rumbled.

Skylar's eyes shot around the room, resting on Peggy clearing a table over by the window. "Dad!" Her freckles almost disappeared in the crimson glow. "I've told him I'll take care of everything," she said in a low voice. "He can see the baby whenever he wants. *If* he wants."

Zack swallowed his scathing reply. He would deal with that when they were alone.

Nash cleared his throat. "See, I think Zack might be a little like me. When I asked your mother to leave, it was on the proviso that she leave you kids here. I couldn't bear to be parted from you, any of you."

"Lots of people are single parents," she began. "Statistics say…"

Nash cut her off. "*Not* in this family, girl. You're a

Fortune. I would ask you to consider the implications of that in all you do."

Skylar's eyes widened.

Nash continued in a softer tone. "Just because it's the modern way doesn't mean it's right for everyone."

She glanced meaningfully at Zack. "If you want to be more involved, then you're just going to have to spend more time in the States."

He frowned at her. She seemed to have left the stammer behind, as well.

Then she did something that rocked him to the core. She leaned right back in that age-old pose of pregnant women everywhere, one hand cradling the bottom of her belly and the other moving slowly, lovingly, just under her breasts.

Something slammed in his chest. Man, he'd never wanted to touch something so much.

"Zack?"

Nash's voice cut through his longing. Zack cleared his throat for the second wave of attack. "We can come over two or three times a year. I know you'll want the baby to grow up knowing family."

Skylar's sweet mouth compressed and she huffed out a sigh. He frowned at her, annoyed with himself for being distracted, even charmed by her. "Skylar, I'm offering you marriage. Security. A good life for that baby of ours. There will be no stigma about single parents, or why Daddy doesn't live with you. You and I aren't romantics. We are sensible, well-grounded people. We'll damn well make this work for the sake of the child."

Her mouth still a straight line, she put her nose in the air and looked away.

Nash rested his elbow on the table, his fingers moving through his graying hair. "I wish Patricia were here. She'd know what to say."

Skylar looked at him, concern softening her lips.

"After we talked last night, Sky, I made a couple of calls, to Teddy and another business contact I have in those parts," Nash commented, eliciting startled glances from both of them. "Zack is wealthy, successful at what he does, and if there are any skeletons in his closet, they're so far back, it doesn't matter a damn. He is well liked and respected. He has never been married, has no children. Teddy and Max are behind him one hundred percent. You could do a lot worse, you know."

Skylar looked at him, smudges of betrayal darkening her eyes. "You're talking about the rest of my life here."

Nash's head rolled back, his broad chest rising on a deep inhalation. "Where does it say marriage is forever? Ask me."

Her eyes shone with sympathy. "Oh, Dad. She'll come back. I know she will."

"She will or she won't." Nash sighed and his stern gaze moved to each of them in turn. "But I have bigger things to worry about than two young people who are very well suited, even if they don't know it yet." He leaned forward and put his hand on his daughter's shoulder. "Love grew for me and Patricia. It didn't happen overnight. Now you have a baby to think of and a family name that has been besmirched once too often for my liking. And I'd like to tell you differently, girl, but there are no guarantees in this life."

Zack watched Skylar's face fall. He actually felt a pang of sympathy for her, even though her father was on his side. But he kept silent. This salvo was between her and Nash.

"Just tell me you'll think about it. Don't set your mind against it on some girlish notion." He put both hands on the table and pushed himself up, sadness evident in his stooped shoulders. "Give me something good to tell Patricia if she calls. She's got a real soft spot for you. She'd love to see you expecting. A marriage in the family is just what's needed to bring us all together again."

"That's blackmail," Skylar whispered.

"Whatever works for you," Nash said comfortably. "Just promise you'll consider it, Skylar. It's not a bad proposition." He turned to Zack, putting out his hand. "Shall I tell Peggy to air out the empty apartment upstairs? No sense wasting time and money on a hotel."

Zack shook his hand. "Maybe in a few days. I'd appreciate it."

The silence lasted minutes after Nash walked heavily from the room. Zack was torn, wanting to comfort her, guessing she felt let down. The temptation was there to go in for the kill while she was vulnerable, the words of her father fresh in her mind. But sometimes, as in business, it was best to let the opposing party lead and hang themselves.

"You can stop looking so smug," she muttered, suddenly, drawing herself up in a tense line.

Her eyes flashed, warming his blood. How could he have forgotten the fire in her? He recalled having the skin of his back raked when he'd realized she was a virgin and momentarily pulled back. That straightened his spine and made him grin. No way would spitfire Skylar allow that!

Catching her eye, he arranged a more sober expression on his face and put his hands behind his head.

"What are you looking at?"

"It occurs to me I've been a bit insensitive."

"Really?" Her mouth curved in what she probably meant to be a sneer, but Skylar's mouth didn't *do* sneer. It was still a sweet smile.

"So I'm asking. Skylar Fortune, will you marry me?"

The indignation drained out of her. Her eyes were troubled, her mouth turned down. "Oh, Zack."

He leaned toward her, taking one of her hands before she could pull back. "It's not the perfect start, I give you that. But a child should have two parents. We are responsible, independently wealthy, sexually compatible…" He smiled at the blush scooting up her throat and face. "And we like each other. We always did."

Skylar bit her lip briefly, drawing his eye. In lieu of kissing her there, where she was so troubled, he raised her hand, laced their fingers together and kissed the tips of hers.

"It's not enough," she mumbled.

He nodded reassuringly. "It's enough."

She squeezed his hand. "Zack, I never ever expected to get pregnant. And I never expected to fall in love and get married and walk off into the sunset, either. But why should you settle for second best?"

"I don't consider you second best," he admonished. "Far from it."

Skylar pulled back from him suddenly, wrapping her arms about her torso. This was all moving too fast. He was too easy, calm, while she felt like screaming and gnashing her teeth. She knew a hustle when she saw one. Her father and Zack were bonding together…and she had a fair idea of what her brothers would think about all of this. Case and Creed, her half brothers, were carbon copies of their father. The scandal this pregnancy would cause would be their main concern. She imagined lots of male posturing and talk of dragging Zack down the aisle.

Gulping air, she rocked back and forth, trying to quell a rising panic. "Oh, I don't know what to say…" she wailed, not caring that Peggy was still in the room.

"Say *yes*, Skylar." Zack's voice remained calm and constant. "I won't let you down."

Why should she believe him? She'd always felt so apart from everyone, like an afterthought. Did no one else see how impossible this was?

It had hurt to hear her father's glib words, passing her fears off like she didn't know her own mind. No guarantees, do what's right, don't surrender to girlish notions…such as love?

A tear welled up. A tear! Skylar Fortune didn't cry. She swiped at her eyes, succeeding only in dislodging it and starting its journey. "He can't force me," she said through clenched teeth. "*You* can't force me. I need the time to make my own decision."

His easy smile and dimples faded. She saw disappointment in his face where, a second ago, victory had lurked. He thought she'd just go along, do as she was told. Skylar didn't make waves, hell, not even a ripple. Everyone would no doubt think she'd be lucky to snare him.

"Don't you think we've wasted enough time?"

She met his accusatory glare and upped it. He wasn't easy now, but he'd backed her into a corner and, like one of her stallions, she was apt to kick.

"If you'd informed me a couple of months ago," Zack said tightly, "we'd have had all the time in the world to get to know each other."

"What difference does it make?" Skylar demanded. "Two months, five months, nine…why do we have to decide about marriage right now?"

Something in his gray eyes shifted. "My baby will not be born illegitimate."

The quiet intensity of his words, each carefully enunciated, the warning in his eyes, made the air throb between them. Skylar inhaled, almost afraid to speak. This wasn't the Zack she knew.

Then he blinked and she couldn't be sure she had seen anything. He was still grim, but he was Zack. New Zealander. Razor-sharp businessman. Vintner and new studmaster.

Sexy. Charming. Considerate.

Father of her baby.

Skylar sighed. She wanted him, she had from the first. But not this way. Not shackled to him because of a broken condom. "I can't give you an answer right…"

"When?" he demanded, cutting her off.

Her jacket rustled with the rise of her shoulders. It was hard not to be disappointed when the intensity he had just displayed suggested it was more the baby he was concerned with, not her. She raised her chin and put some steel into her spine.

Zack inhaled. "I'll have to go home for a few days to sort out some things." He frowned down at the table. "Make arrangements for a longer absence. We need to spend time together, Skylar."

Or then again…Skylar nodded hopefully, her breath hitching when he reached for her hand.

"This is my first baby, too," he told her, his tone softer now. "I want to be there for it. The whole thing."

Or maybe not. Her shoulders dropped, but at least

she would have some peace, some thinking time. "I'm not going anywhere."

Zack suddenly pulled her toward him, squeezing her fingers firmly. "I want you to swear, on the baby's life, that you'll not do anything stupid while I'm gone."

Her heart lurched. "Wh-what?"

"Like run," Zack grated, "hide. Let your family talk you into getting rid of the baby."

"They wouldn't…I would never…"

She was shocked that he could even *think* that…from the instant she had first felt pregnant, that was an option that had never entered her head.

"Swear, Skylar." Zack's grip was just short of painful. "I have no intention of losing this baby."

"Zack, I would rather die than…"

"I won't be cut out of this, do you understand?" His voice was low, almost menacing. "I may not be quite in the league of the Dakota Fortunes but I've got enough behind me to make things very nasty, and very public, if you do anything to hurt my child. Do you understand?"

Skylar nodded woodenly. "I swear."

Well, at least everyone knew where they stood. Zack Manning had no interest in her. It was the baby he wanted. She was only the incubator.

A movement over his shoulder caught her eye and Skylar stiffened and snatched her hand from his.

Three

A clawing tension descended as Maya Blackstone walked into the room. Skylar straightened her spine, folding her arms protectively around her middle.

"Hi." Ever curious, Maya scooted around to the side and beamed when she saw who was sitting with Skylar. "Zack! I didn't know you were back."

"Gidday, Maya." Zack slowly got to his feet, a genuine smile on his face. "Just leaving actually, but I'll be back in a few days." The smile faded as he turned back to Skylar. "Take good care, Skylar. You have my number."

He nodded at the two women and walked out.

"Want something to eat?" Skylar felt almost giddy with relief at his leaving, though that was tempered by the knowledge she now had the task of telling everyone about the baby. At least she could do that her own way, without Zack breathing down her neck.

Maya shook her head. "I'm relieved to hear you talk about food," she said, looking thoughtfully after Zack. "Since you missed our last two dinner dates."

Maya didn't come to the house if she could help it so they usually got together once a month at her place in town.

"What brings you here?"

"I came to see if there was any word on Mom. Blake tells me Nash has hired an investigator."

Blake! He should be first to know, really. She owed him, Skylar thought darkly, for instigating Zack's visit. And then there was her mother…

Sensing she was the object of avid attention, Skylar looked up into Maya's curious face.

"So, the handsome Kiwi is back. How do you feel about that?"

May as well get it over with. While she was choosing her words, Maya tilted her head and narrowed her eyes.

"Don't tell me, I can see. Your usual slobby attire aside, you look great, Skylar. The picture of health."

She blinked, frowning. "What do you mean, slobby? These jeans are only a year old."

Her friend grinned. "Come on. You wear your clothes like a shield." Her nicely manicured fingers flicked toward the front of Skylar's jacket. "Your wardrobe could do with a complete overhaul."

"Excuse me for living," Skylar protested. "Just because Eliza is in Montana with Reese doesn't mean you have to take over as chief nag." At least she was spared being dragged all over town to replace her wardrobe and having her half sister camped on her doorstep, making sure she took care of herself.

Anyway, back to the task at hand. Skylar hadn't told

her best friend she'd slept with Zack, though she had mentioned liking him—a lot. "Maya, do you remember the night of Case's wedding?"

Maya nodded. "The night Eliza got her wish and finally talked you into a dress."

What a monumental disaster that turned out to be. "And later you barged into the cottage after the fight with Creed?"

Maya's mouth compressed. Creed was the main reason she didn't like coming to the house, Skylar suspected. Those two brought out the worst in each other.

"Maya, I was," she cleared her throat self-consciously "*with* Zack. That night in the cottage."

It should have been funny, the openmouthed gape, the dawning horror, but for the life of her, Skylar could not dredge up a smile.

"I didn't…" Maya stammered, "Oh, no, please, tell me I didn't interrupt…"

Skylar shook her head glumly. "We made it to the finish line. Just."

Maya flopped back in her chair, blowing out a long puff of air. "So it's official. I am now the only virgin left in all of South Dakota."

Skylar didn't smile. In fact, for the first time since she'd had the pregnancy confirmed, she put her face in her hands and burst into tears, shocking them both.

Six days later, Skylar heard the screaming from her office and leapt to her feet. Without even knowing how she got there, she hurtled in through the entrance of the stallion barn, yelling for the grooms, then abruptly skidded to a halt.

The main stable housing the twenty-five broodmares

she accommodated was ten meters away and most of the mares were out in the pasture, enjoying the spring weather for a few hours. The stallion barn had four stalls, two on one side opening out onto handsome landscaped gardens and a lane that forked and led to two grassed yards, set diagonally apart. The other two stalls opened into the breezeway. That way, even when the stallions were both in residence, they didn't have to see each other or be led past the other's stall.

Demetrius, a large fourteen-year-old chestnut, had stood at Fortune Stud for two and a half years. He was middle of the road, his crop placing quite regularly on the track. He was not particularly unruly for a stallion, but when Skylar purchased the prized Black Power a year ago, Deme resented the young usurper. Hence the modified barn. They may have to room together but they did not have to like looking at each other.

Demetrius wasn't in his box. Over the years, he'd caused great amusement by nudging and nibbling on the bolt of the top Dutch door to his stall until he opened it. Deme's party trick, they called it, and everyone took special care to check the bottom half was securely latched after mucking out or returning him to his stall.

Both the top and bottom halves of the door were wide-open. An ominous bashing from inside Black Power's stall down the end told her that her most valuable asset was in trouble. Skylar spun and raced down the outside of the barn.

As she feared, the big chestnut had gone visiting. His ears were back and he lunged his head and neck inside the open top door of the stall. A crunching bang from inside, accompanied by a high-pitched roar drowned out Skylar's renewed calls for help. Demetrius lunged again, showing his teeth. She glimpsed a flash of black as Ace, Black Power's stable name, reared up in his prison, his legs flailing in the air around Deme's head.

"Deme, no!" She leapt toward the horses, wincing when one of Black Power's legs pounded against the top of the door.

Suddenly an iron grip on her arm hauled her sharply back against a hard wall of muscle.

"No!" Zack Manning said in a low snarl. "Get back." His eyes blazing, he yanked her roughly to the side of him. "Stay."

Air jetted from her lungs as she lurched to a standstill.

Stripping off his suit jacket, he flung it at her and began rolling his shirtsleeves up. "Deme, right?" He jerked his head toward the two horses. He'd met both back in January.

"Careful, he can be…"

Zack gave her a scathing look. "Get outta here. Find someone to help, *now*." He advanced toward the stallion.

Skylar raced back into the stallion barn to look for a lead and yelled again for Bob, the head groom. Hearing voices, she stuck her head out the door. Her four workers were walking back from the mare's barn. Urging them to hurry, she rushed back to Zack with them hot on her heels.

Zack had a tight hand on Deme's halter and was bringing his head down. She saw his lips moving, talking, soothing. The others moved slowly around the horse. She gave the lead to Bob and watched with relief as he clipped it on to the halter. Deme gave another toss of the head and finally was coaxed into taking a backward step.

Her attention was on the stall now. There was another crunching blow that shook the building. Skylar covered her mouth with her hand and prayed. Ace was ten million dollars' worth of horse, syndicated to the Fortunes and two other parties. Skylar's biggest gamble, and he was due to serve a mare in less than two hours. The standing fee for this seven-year-old stallion was twelve thousand dollars. *Please, God, don't let him hurt himself.*

Her growing reputation amongst breeders in this part of the States was mostly due to the huge investment in Ace. He was a young sire but with fine lineage and his first crop two years ago was already making an impact on sales all over the States.

Bob, the head groom and stallion manager, released Deme into the care of the others and stepped up to the stall. Ace was still playing up, smashing up the stall. Skylar took a couple of anxious steps forward but Zack moved in front of her, shouldering her away. He stood next to Bob who leaned into the Dutch door, talking quietly to the agitated beast.

Her relief overwhelmed her but she wouldn't be satisfied until she'd had a good look at her pride and joy. She stretched and strained behind the two men, subsiding when Zack flicked her a scornful glance before turning his back again.

Frustrated, she bent and scooped up his suit jacket. His arrival had been a surprise. All she'd known for sure was he'd be here before the weekend. She had expected him to phone with more specifics. She hadn't expected him to just show up at the stable, still in his business suit.

Bob was still talking to Ace. She stood behind them restlessly, trying to peer between Zack's broad shoulders and the older man's tall, thin form. Standing on tiptoe, she caught flashes of a sweat-darkened flank as the stallion paced and blew, trembling with rage and fear.

"Is he all right?"

"Let's give him a few minutes," Bob muttered, "till he's calmed some."

Zack turned abruptly and took her arm. "What the hell were you thinking?" he muttered, propelling her a few feet away.

The adrenaline drained away, leaving impatience and a feeling of defensiveness. "What was I supposed to do? Let him kick himself to…"

"Get help," he grated.

Skylar frowned at him from under the peak of her cap. "Do you know how much he's worth?"

Zack stepped up to her, close. She was not short, being five foot nine in her stocking feet, but she sure felt small with his lean body, rigid in anger, looming over her.

"Not as much as that baby you're carrying," he said in a deceptively soft voice. "The one you swore an oath to protect."

Her head dropped. He was right—she should never have gone near the stall. It was instinct driving her. In all honesty, and it was hard to admit it even to herself, she had completely forgotten about being pregnant when she'd heard the screams of the sparring stallions.

"I know. I'm sorry. I just didn't think—"

Zack glared down at her. "That's the last time you don't think. Starting now, you don't go near these horses, any of them."

Her head snapped up and she roasted him with a

scowl that matched his own. This was a new side to him, and Skylar didn't like it one bit. "It's the busiest time of the year…" she bit out, struggling to hold her temper. Another surprise since she didn't think she had a temper to hold.

"We'll manage." Zack's eyes were like granite and he stood, legs braced, like an immovable force. "Won't we, Bob?"

How dare he undermine her authority like that? She heard Bob's grunt, saw his large ears turn pink and recognized he'd made the judicious decision not to turn his head.

"I have to call the vet," she muttered, wrenching her arm from his grip. Okay, she was sorry, but when all was said and done, nothing had happened. She and the baby were fine. Pebbles erupted in angry little spurts under her boots as she stomped off toward her office.

Who did he think he was? He and her cousin Max had come to *her* for help a few months ago, not the other way around. This was her life's work, for Pete's sake! Lost in a spiteful exchange that was only in her head, she was suddenly aware he had followed when her office door banged with enough force to rattle the windows.

"While we're on it," he said, striding up to her desk, "that goes for riding, too. Till after the baby is born."

Skylar stopped like a slap and turned slowly to face him. "What?"

He leaned back, folding his arms.

"Zack, I can handle horses. I've been riding since I could walk."

"I ride, too," he said evenly. "When's the last time a horse shied on you?"

Her lips parted with a scathing retort. Like a flash, the remembered pain of being dumped unceremoniously on her rear end a few months ago sent the retort up in a puff of smoke. Her hand crept behind her and she gave her backside a quick rub. Roscoe, her ancient gelding, had never liked surprises and a well-camouflaged snake slithering over a log certainly surprised him that day.

Skylar's shoulders slumped and she gave the unkempt surface of her desk a thorough scrutiny. She was honest enough to admit to receiving her fair share of bruises, even broken bones, over the years from shying horses.

With a downcast face, she saw Zack's fingers relax a little where they curled around his biceps.

Skylar sank down into her chair. "Is this what it's going to be like?" she asked quietly.

There was no answer, forcing her to look up.

"Demanding this…demanding that?"

"Horses are unpredictable."

"I meant you. Not asking. Not talking, just…"

"Where the safety of the baby is concerned, yes." He punctuated that with a nod, then unfolded his arms and sat. "I'm still learning but you showed me your system in January. With your supervision, from here—" he waved a hand around her office "—and Bob in charge, me and the boys will keep things running smoothly."

"We're still covering most days. The summer mares are arriving and there are still half a dozen late foals to come."

"Well, it'll be good practice for me when we kick off in our spring." His tone and gaze did not waver. "Skylar, this is difficult for both of us."

She nodded sullenly, tapping her desk.

"We need to spend time together, get to know each

other. That means I'll be here every day under your feet. It would be easier if you'd give us a chance."

Irritated by her tapping fingers, she twisted her hands together. "I don't like being given orders."

"I'm not an unreasonable man. I'll listen to your arguments and concerns. But I won't let you take any chances with our baby."

Our baby. He was right, she supposed. This life inside her was precious and fragile, and although she'd like to tell him to mind his own business, this was his business.

She rocked forward, still clasping her hands together. "I guess I can understand that."

There was a long silence while she swallowed her resentment, let her mind concede that his requests and demands were not so unreasonable. She had already relinquished a lot of her more physical workload over the last weeks in deference to her pregnancy.

"You look good, Skylar. Are you?"

She nodded. Now that the morning sickness had passed, she felt energized by a feeling of well-being and good health. Her mouth softened, remembering yesterday's ride on Roscoe down by the lake. She'd dropped the reins and just buried her face in his mane, arms around his neck, chattering like a moron. Just because she needed to share the exhilaration, the burgeoning love for this tiny life inside, even if it was just with an old horse.

Could she share with him, the father of her baby? Skylar wanted to, but she didn't know how to take this grim stranger. He was so different from the attentive, respectful man she had fallen for a few months ago.

Zack's impending return had filled her with a mixture of excitement and trepidation. Would a week see him reconciled to the pregnancy, more reasonable about his insistence on marriage to a virtual stranger?

If today was anything to go by, she was inclined to think not.

Zack arched his spine, acknowledging his body's exhaustion. He'd crossed umpteen time zones in the last week between the States, New Zealand and Australia and then back to the States. There were arrangements to make for an indefinite absence from his substantial franchise conglomerate. Luckily his winemaker had completed harvesting in Zack's absence and there wasn't much going on at the new stud right now as the foaling and breeding seasons were the opposite of the northern hemisphere. Managing the weanlings comprised the main business at this time of year.

He looked down at his three-hundred-dollar shirt and the expensive suit pants that were now streaked with horse sweat and dust. It was fair to say it hadn't been a good week.

The rage seeped away but there was enough residue to narrow his eyes when he looked at her. It would take a while to get over seeing the expectant mother of his baby walking up to twelve hundred pounds of loose and agitated horseflesh.

But she did look good, more magnificently pregnant than a week ago. There was no mistaking it now.

A wave of fatigue made him light-headed. Every muscle, every sinew, had jumped to attention and been stretched to the limit. It was adrenaline, jet lag and a measure of stress. He was dead on his feet.

"The doctors are happy?" It was an effort to un-
clench his jaw.

She nodded, relaxing a little.

"How did your family take the news?"

Skylar sucked on her bottom lip gently then released
it with a small smacking noise. "With varying degrees
of amazement."

That's what her brother had told him when he
phoned two days ago. Zack respected Blake's direct-
ness. He was almost friendly once satisfied of Zack's
intention to marry his sister and that he had no interest
in milking the family's coffers. He even suggested they
double up, as he and his fiancée, Sasha, were planning
a winter wedding.

Blake had also warned him to tread carefully with
Trina, his and Skylar's mother. Apparently she liked
to meddle in the Fortune's affairs, even to the extent of
supplying the tabloids with false information about her
own children.

"What about yours?" Skylar asked.

His head raised. The jury was still out on how much
to divulge about a rather unusual family situation with
his soon-to-be wife. "Surprised," he told her. "But in-
creasingly happy about becoming a granddad."

She looked as if she expected more. Less was more,
especially concerning his father. "He's not in the picture much."

"Is your mother…"

Zack nodded. "She died four years ago after a long
illness." He paused, watching her face carefully. "They
hadn't been together for some time." What would she
feel about that? Skylar Fortune was, after all, a horse
breeder. Lineage was important to her, although her own
parents did not have a great track record in that respect.

He found only honest curiosity there. Her clear skin and eyes, the slight parting of her wide, shapely lips had him struggling to believe what Blake had let slip on the phone. It was an innocent enough comment, but it confirmed Zack's suspicions that he was set up four months ago at the wedding. Set up for seduction by this innocent-looking woman.

Why? Was it just about the baby? Did she want the baby, not the man?

He hardened his heart. No one, not Skylar nor her wealthy family was going to cut him out of his baby's life and run him out of town.

He exhaled and pushed himself slowly to his feet. "I'm beat. I'll see you tomorrow. Do the boys log on at six or…"

Skylar nodded.

"So you get to sleep in," he commented, picking up his jacket.

"It's not necessary, Zack." She rose also. "The boys can manage. They've been doing so for the last few weeks, mostly."

"Shall I walk you back to the cottage?"

She declined. "I have some calls to make. I think I'll postpone Ace's cover this afternoon. I can't risk him hurting a mare. And I'll get the vet out to have a look."

"Don't you go near him," Zack warned.

She shook her head. "I won't. Are you staying up at the big house?"

Zack's eyes moved slowly over her. "I'm open to a better offer."

She rewarded him with a blush. "How long will you stay?"

"Depends on you. But just so you know, we have weeks, not months, Skylar. I have pressing business commitments right now."

Her shoulders drooped and she looked away.

This wasn't the way it was meant to be. Their reunion should have been pleasant. So far he'd given her ten different reasons to turn him down. But he was tired. He was angry for what she'd put him through today and for the inadvertent comment Blake had made on the phone. He was deeply worried that his own father was spinning wheels on the other side of the world that would have a devastating impact here.

A yawn caught him unawares. Zack was in no shape to go five rounds about a wedding right now. It would be enough to make the ten-minute walk up to the house without collapsing. "Don't reject us without giving it a go," he murmured, then hoisted his jacket and felt the lump in the pocket. "Here's a DVD I made of my home and the vineyard and the stud. Forgive the quality—I haven't had much practice at home movies." He handed her the disc and headed for the door, his head spinning with exhaustion.

Four

"I did not!" Skylar's voice rose in indignation. There was no way she'd canceled the Clendon mare.

Her head groom, Bob Keen, slid his cap back and scratched his forehead.

"What did he say, exactly?"

Bob had called the Nebraskan breeder when the maiden mare hadn't arrived as arranged.

"That a woman phoned yesterday claiming to be you and left a message that Black Power's season was cut short because of a paddock accident."

Skylar shook her head in bewilderment. "That's baloney. I postponed his afternoon serve because of Deme's little stint but I definitely haven't canceled anyone." She sighed. "I'd better call him."

"Don't bother," Bob told her, rising. "He's already

made other arrangements. She's been palpated and she's ready to go. He didn't want to risk waiting."

Dammit, she was looking forward to doing business with the man from Omaha. His broodmares were well regarded and he rarely dealt with stud farms outside a select two or three in Kentucky. His approach was made on the recommendation of another Nebraskan breeder. Whatever the misunderstanding was, it left her operation looking less than professional.

"While you're here," she said to Bob as he turned to go, "did you find out who left Deme's stall unlatched yesterday?"

Bob sighed heavily and screwed his face up. "Could've been any one of us," he said in his slow drawl.

Skylar gave him a skeptical look as he left her office, knowing he wouldn't rat on one of the boys. It was worth mentioning only because she needed to remind everyone she was still the boss around here. Truthfully, she hadn't been pulling her weight since she'd learned she was pregnant.

But she wasn't overly worried. She trusted in Bob's authority. Whoever left that latch open would hear it from the sharp end of his tongue and it would be a whole lot worse than if she said anything.

Hearing voices, she wandered over to the window, not for the first time today. It had only been one morning and Skylar was sick of four walls already. The allure of paperwork lost its appeal while *he* was barely ten feet away, bending his long back over a shovel or broom, bantering with the boys.

Zack Manning looked like he'd slept well. Looked like he belonged here, mucking out stables, leading the horses out to pasture, washing down the mares for their stints in the receiving barn. She strained her ears as the unfamiliar accent drifted in through her open window, startlingly different from the other men's lazy drawling dialect.

One thing was plain: the boys liked him. Everybody did, including her family. Most likely they were surprised that he'd even bothered with her, let alone want to sleep with her.

Certainly no one had thought to ask what she wanted. All the talk centered on weddings and reputations. Her family was probably fearful that, if she didn't hurry up, she'd lose the only guy who would ever ask her.

Dragging her jacket on, she chose an apple from the fruit bowl on her desk—apples were her only craving so far—and decided to stretch her legs. Zack looked up from his shoveling, midsentence, and watched her pass.

"Keep your shirt on, Manning," she said snippily as she breezed past the men in the yard. "I'm just going to give old Roscoe a treat." Ignoring the curious stares of the grooms, she tugged the peak of her cap down and must have even tossed her head, because her long braid thumped on her back a couple of times.

Behind her, Zack said something to Ben, the youngest and newest member of her team of workers. She heard a snort of laughter then the clang of a shovel hitting the fence. Her heartbeat ratcheted up a notch when she sensed determined footfalls coming after her but she did not slow.

Roscoe raised his head and ambled toward her. She took out her pocket knife and began to cut the apple into slices, taking a bite from one.

"How old is he?" Zack's frame leaned on the fence beside her.

"Twenty-one."

The old bay blew softly as he drew near and rubbed his face and ear against the fence, inviting a scratch from Zack.

"Since I'm not allowed to ride, I hope you figured in some exercise for old Roscoe here." That would teach him for being so dictatorial, she thought, amused. "A bit of a jog for an hour every other day should do it."

"Ben's lighter," Zack pointed out.

"Ben only has one speed, flat-out."

There was a burst of laughter from the men over by the stable. Skylar looked around. The three faces were turned their way.

"It's about me being the father."

"You *told* them?"

He shrugged. "I confirmed it. They'd noticed you…" his eyes flicked down to her midriff "…weren't yourself and they're wondering what I'm doing here." It was his turn to sound amused.

"What's so funny?" she demanded, her eyes still on the men.

Zack exhaled. "I told Ben to spread the word. If any of them see you near a loose horse," he paused "shoot the damn horse."

Skylar's eyes shot back to his face. He hadn't smiled but there was a sparkle in his eyes as he squinted into the midmorning sun. She decided not to give him the satisfaction of a response so she turned back to slicing the apple and offering it to Roscoe. Her old faithful had his nose buried in Zack's sleeve, eyes closed in bliss as his ears were given a good old-fashioned scratch.

She sighed. Just because every living thing on this estate had taken a shine to Zack Manning didn't mean she had to go along. Holding out the apple, she took three or four steps along the fence, coaxing Roscoe toward the new automatic livestock waterer. "Come on, boy, have a drink." He hated freezing cold water so she'd given him a treat and had his own heated water trough installed.

"What are you up to today?" Zack asked, taking a slice of fruit from her fingers and offering it·to the horse.

"I'm going into town shortly. I've got some grain and stuff to pick up."

"Want some help?"

"Nope." She needed a few things that weren't exactly on her supply list.

"Don't you be lifting…"

"I won't," she told him quickly, turning to reassure him.

He was closer than expected when their eyes met. Skylar sucked in a breath, unprepared for the shake-up her nerve endings were getting.

It was not the first time. Her quick slide into a one-sided magnum crush began in January when she, Zack and Max, her Australian cousin a couple of times removed, had spent a few days flying around the Midwest. They were looking at horses for a stud farm the two men were setting up in New Zealand. Had he guessed of her infatuation? Was he planning to railroad her into something she wasn't ready for by laying on the charm?

She recalled the first time she'd met her cousin after Nash and Patricia had told the Australian Fortunes of her small breeding operation. They hit if off immediately, with Max ribbing her unmercifully from day one. She enjoyed his irreverent and quirky humor and, if Zack hadn't been there, would have given as good as she got.

But he *was* there, quiet, alert, respectful. From what Max said, he was a sharp businessman who had amassed a fortune in a very few years. His desire to learn the breeding business and admiration for her knowledge was enough of an attraction from the start.

But Skylar's uncharacteristic fascination with his dimples, watchful eyes, muscular build should have set the alarm bells clanging. They were forever in close quarters—tiny planes, stalls, cabs. Just a couple of days into their visit, she morphed into a breathless, red-faced wreck every time he looked at her. The instances where they brushed hands or arms nearly paralyzed her.

Like now. He watched her as if he knew the hairs were doing the quickstep on the back of her neck.

"I, um, better go," she stammered, pushing the remaining fruit into Roscoe's soft nose.

"Let's get together later."

"Wh-why?" God, she was such an idiot.

Zack sighed, his eyes on her face. "Talk. Drink coffee. Get to know each other."

"Oh. At my place?"

He nodded.

Okay, she could handle that…if she kept reminding herself it was her turf.

"Did you watch the DVD last night?"

She wiped the blade of the pocket knife and closed it. "You have a…" she shrugged, not used to giving compliments, "…nice home." Maybe tonight would be a great idea, serve as an icebreaker. "And some beautiful horses." Reminded, she smiled at her drooling, chomping pet. "Who lives there with you?"

"Just me."

That was a lot of house for one person. "Where does your father live?"

"Not far away, but don't worry. He's not on the doorstep every five minutes."

Why should she be worried? "No brothers or sisters?"

He shook his head. Roscoe nibbled on his sleeve while he told her about the skiing and beaches all within a half hour of the valley and the nearby city of Christchurch, a couple of times the size of Sioux Falls.

"A city in training," he said with a smile. "But there're theatres and nightclubs, if that's your bent, and plenty of good eating places. There are some closer smaller towns. You don't have to go far for supplies, whether for entertaining or business."

"Do you entertain a lot?" She was so unsophisticated. Her relations, especially Eliza, were much more comfortable in social situations than she was.

Zack grinned. "Yeah, it's pretty racy. We have a Christmas party for the workers and other farmers around the district. It's the talk of the tabloids for months."

Skylar broke into a reluctant smile. She liked him so much…the old feelings returned full force. "Front-page news, right?"

He reached out and slapped the old horse on the flank. "I had my share of action when Max and I were out conquering the world. About three years ago, I'd had enough of the rat race and public attention and retired myself to the quiet country life."

"Are you and Max famous?"

"He's a lot more famous, or infamous, than I am. We

have had some spectacular successes over the years and one or two gigantic failures. I'm not unknown down in my neck of the woods but it's fairly unobtrusive." He paused. "Would you miss that? Being gossiped about?"

Her braid flopped over her shoulder as she shook her head. "No, sir. Though I haven't exactly set the papers on fire." Skylar looked down and caught sight of her bulge pushing out under her jacket. *Until now,* she amended silently.

"Publicity can be a double-edged sword," Zack said, his expression becoming serious. He fell silent, looking out over the pasture.

Skylar picked up her supplies then parked her car in the shopping district, intending to spend ten minutes refreshing her wardrobe. With an armful of low-waisted jeans, bib overalls and large-sized T-shirts, she headed for the checkout but paused at a rack of spring dresses. Some of the colors were out of this world, not that she would have a clue what suited her. "Where are you, when I need you, Eliza?" she muttered under her breath, It wouldn't hurt to try a couple on, especially as she was now effectively an office worker.

Some time later, she found herself in the beauty salon. Trying on dresses was all very well but it was painfully obvious that the last—and first time—she'd had her legs waxed was Case and Gina's wedding.

It made good use of time to allow Roz to fuss with her hair while she was there, clucking over its dry condition. Things escalated from there. There wasn't much she could do while the foul smelling foil-tips color developed so she did not demur at the suggestion of a manicure and pedicure. "It's a slow day," Roz told her, "lucky for you."

Two and a half hours later and several hair shades lighter, she emerged from the salon, tingling all over. Luckily there was an old rubber band in the lining of her pocket, so with that and her cap, she was able to hide a lot of the damage. But on the way to the car, she passed the boutique Eliza had dragged her into the week before Case's wedding.

The dress in the window was the most fantastic shade of russet. She stood there gawking for so long that the assistant came to the door.

"Nice to see you again, Ms. Fortune."

Skylar mumbled something as she was drawn into the shop, unable to take her eyes off that dress.

"That burnt sienna color would look gorgeous on you. How did the jade outfit go a few months ago? Your brother's wedding, wasn't it?"

Eliza obviously shopped here a lot for this woman to remember her one encounter with Skylar.

The woman slid the dress off the hanger. "Do you have a strapless bra?"

She couldn't help sniggering. Luckily, the boutique carried a range of designer undergarments. This day was turning into a roller coaster she seemed unable to stop. Why was she doing it? Did she want to make herself more attractive for him?

"I need new clothes, that's all," she muttered, patting her bulge. "Nothing fits."

The assistant's eyes lit up.

Much later, she slid her battered black leather wallet into her back pocket and hurried to the car before her credit card vomited all over her purchases. At home, it took two trips to lug all the bags upstairs. She dumped them unceremoniously onto her bed and flopped down herself. "Impossible," she moaned, kicking off her Doc Martens and rubbing her nicely pedicured but aching feet. Some women actually found shopping pleasurable. Apparently, pregnant women left their modesty at the door. Skylar's tingling-all-over body reminded her that a great deal of it had been stripped, scrutinized and sometimes painfully attended to today.

A knock at the door galvanized her. Checking that not too much weird-smelling hair showed under her cap, she hurried downstairs, wondering if her depleted eyebrows still looked as surprised as they felt. If he said so much as a word…

Zack leaned on the door, tilting his head to peer at her face. "You've done something to your hair."

Skylar heaved a sigh. "Just a trim," she lied and stalked into the kitchen without extending an invitation. It was difficult to walk normally after a bikini wax, another first.

Zack watched while she self-consciously made some coffee. She wasn't used to being watched. Wasn't used to any of this. Her nose twitched at the delicious aroma of his real coffee. Instant decaf just wasn't the same.

He sat at her kitchen table and she brought the drinks over and cleared a place amidst the clutter.

Zack's eyes followed the progress of a book she tossed on top of the pile and his tan seemed to fade. He reached across and picked it up. "Baby names," he read before looking up into her face.

A rush of embarrassment heated her skin. "It's a little early for that, I know," she mumbled.

He exhaled slowly. "I haven't given it any thought." He searched her face. "Have you?"

"Not really."

"Do you know what sex it is?"

No, and that suited her fine. "I had a scan last week but I asked them not to tell me. Do you want to see the picture?" She rose and found the ultrasound picture in a drawer in the kitchen. Zack's eyes widened when she placed it in front of him. It was a long time before he looked up again.

Skylar studied his earnest expression over the rim of her cup, feeling guilty. Last week it had occurred to her to reschedule the scan so he could attend but her nerve failed her. The image of lying spread out and bare bellied in front of him was way too personal for the current status of their relationship. If it *was* a relationship.

He shrugged helplessly. "You'll have to show me."

Skylar scooted her chair closer, not close enough to touch him, and pointed out all the important bits.

After a long time, Zack leaned back and put his hands behind his head but his eyes remained on the photo. "How often do they do the ultrasound?"

She stood and moved her chair back to the head of the table. "That's it unless there are problems." To avoid witnessing the disappointment on his face, she transferred her attention to sorting through a stack of mail on the table.

"Speaking of doctors," he finally looked up at her face, "I had the works done while I was home last week. Blood tests, HIV, X-rays and a complete history. There is nothing genetic for us to be worried about."

That was something she had not even considered. She opened her mouth to tell him she had no idea about her family genetics when he fixed her with a very intense look.

"That means I'm safe."

The air whistled in through her nostrils and she blinked and looked away. Sex. He was referring to sex, between them, in the future. Unprotected sex…

Her heart started thumping.

Zack's mouth dried. He knew when a woman was thinking about sex, with him. He'd seen this before from her, months ago. But then she changed the game plan after the event. Backed off and closed up completely.

He supposed that to a woman, especially a shy woman like Skylar, her first time would be a lot to process. So despite his surprise and disappointment, he'd allowed her to avoid him the day after they'd made love. But then he got called home urgently and did not even get the opportunity to say goodbye. Instead he made plans to return later in the year for the Keeneland sales in Kentucky, knowing that she and Nash always attended. He kept in contact by phone and decided that, unless he met someone else that touched him the way she did, he would push matters then.

Circumstances had changed. Whether by accident or design, she was carrying his child. No one would run him off this time.

What had Blake said? That she must have set her cap for him that night because no one had ever seen her take the slightest interest in her appearance before. The whole family had been as shocked as he was when she walked into the wedding reception looking so glamorous.

If this whole thing was a plan to get him into bed and get pregnant, why not tell him as soon as she knew about the baby? Unless a baby was the prize she coveted. The objective.

Zack did not have the time to be considerate and patient. "The night of Case's wedding," he said, watching her closely. "Did you plan it so we'd end up together?"

Her cornflower-blue gaze skittered away from his face. "Not planned, exactly." Her fingers twisted together. "Hoped, maybe."

There was guilt all over her face. Even her eyebrows looked inflamed. "Is this what you wanted, Skylar? Was I just the means to an end?"

She did look at him then, a real look, not the usual over-the-left-shoulder look. "It was your condom, Zack," she told him softly.

Hell, of course it was. "I know."

Her shoulders jerked. "Dumb luck, that's all." She rubbed her eye with a knuckle and gave a self-deprecating smile. "I can't even get sex right."

She must be joking! Memories of the passion and pleasure they'd shared flashed again in his mind, like a hundred times before. If it wasn't for Maya's untimely arrival— Which reminded him. "Did you forget to lock the door that night or does Maya have a key?" Zack had been so consumed with lust at the time, intent on unlocking much more intimate doors, that he hadn't considered the possibility of an intrusion.

"I hardly ever lock it. It's private land."

He wrenched his thoughts back to the present. "You will from now on," he warned, holding her gaze. "You're too isolated out here between the stables and the house."

He made a mental note to check the lock on the way out. "Independence is one thing, Skylar, but you don't have to go through all this on your own."

Her cheeks puffed out a breath. "Well, now everybody knows, I'm guessing I won't be left on my own for a minute."

He sharpened his look.

Skylar raised her hands. "I only meant that I'm not used to the attention. No one notices me usually. I'm just little Skylar, playing houese with her horses." She wrinkled her nose. "Eeww! That sounded tragic, didn't it?"

"You sure got my attention," he said with feeling.

"How did you see it, my attraction, so quickly, Zack? No one else noticed but you knew straight away."

He'd wondered about that, himself. "It was written all over your face."

She looked down and passed her hand over her eyes. "I was so embarrassed about that night. I couldn't believe it when you called. And kept calling."

"I liked you right from the start, Skylar. You knew that."

"How'm I supposed to know? I've never even had a boyfriend before."

Zack put his elbows on the table and steepled his hands. "And now you're going to be a mother."

"It feels…" She leaned back and laid her hands on her belly. "How can you go your whole life and not know how much you wanted something?" She looked up at him with wonder. "It just feels right."

His eyes glued to her hands. A longing so deep, so wrenching, assailed him. "*This* feels right, Skylar. Us. Come home with me."

Apprehension chased the wonder on her face away. "I want you to be involved, Zack, but you must see that marriage is just too big a step."

"I'll make up for whatever you lose by moving away," he vowed.

"You'll·make up for my family, my business?"

"You just said your family never notices you. As for the horses, you can be equal partners with Max and I. Call it a wedding gift from us both."

"He might have something to say about that."

"Max would be delighted. You'd not be coming empty-handed. With your knowledge and contacts here, we'll make it the best stud operation in the country. Bring Ace, if you want."

"He's syndicated," Skylar mumbled. "It's not just up to me."

"We talked about shuttling him a few months ago and you were all for it. Skylar, we can work all this out later. You write your ticket, your prenup, whatever. Just let's get it done."

She looked up from under her lashes and set her mouth in a stubborn line. "You've got an answer for everything, haven't you? Zack, I need more time."

"If you'd told me earlier of the pregnancy, we could have had all the time in the world. The way things are now, my business commitments don't allow me the time." He inhaled and swallowed the frustration he heard creeping into his tone. "Is this because you haven't had a boyfriend before? You want romance. I can do that, Skylar, after the wedding. But right now, I want you settled and happy well before the baby is born."

"Settled and happy," she murmured, as if to herself. "You know, Zack, you're right. I haven't had much of a love life. I should probably be grateful to you for saving me from certain spinsterhood." His exasperated sigh didn't move her. "And it's true that I like you better than I've ever liked anyone."

She met his eyes now and hers were resolute, reminding him that he would not get things all his way with this woman. Shy little Skylar was growing in more ways than one.

"But I have a baby to consider now. I will be making decisions with this—" her hand moved over the swell of her belly "—foremost in my mind." She jutted out her chin defiantly. "I am Skylar Fortune from South Dakota. You need to give me a bunch of reasons why I should become a New Zealander in such an all-fired rush."

Well, well. She was certainly beggaring his first impressions. Pregnancy had upped her confidence and, although part of him wanted to shake her, his admiration grudgingly grew. "Your own father thinks we have a lot to build on. *I* think we have a lot to build on."

There was a ghost of a smile on her face, but she directed it at her stomach. "That's because I have something you want. At least be honest about it, Zack."

His eyes narrowed. "I *am* being honest about it."

"You're well traveled, sophisticated. Used to going out to nice restaurants and parties and probably have a dozen beautiful women you can call up at anytime. Zack, I'm not one of those women. I'm not like that. This is me." She swept her hands down in front of her. "Not that girl at the wedding."

"I'm not asking you to be the girl at the wedding," Zack argued. "I liked you before that. I think you're gorgeous in jeans, or out of them, for that matter."

She huffed impatiently, flushing. "It's the baby you want, not me."

Zack rose abruptly and leaned over her chair, sliding one arm firmly around her waist. "Are you sure about that, Skylar?" Lifting her so that her backside was right off the seat and only her stocking toes touched the floor, he crushed his lips down on hers.

He remembered her mouth. Wide, sweetly curved and irresistible. Her name smiled through his mind like a warm welcome. He felt again what he had months ago, that she fit. That he wanted to be with her in some way that was important and bewildering. Anticipation was sweet on his tongue.

It took a few seconds but she responded with tentative acceptance. He pulled her more firmly against him and felt her hands clutch at his shoulders and the weight of her body shift, as if she flowed up into him. Desire pumped loudly in his ears and he nearly forgot his purpose. Easy does it, don't scare her, he reminded himself. This is just a taste.

He pulled back from her mouth and opened his eyes. She released a strangled breath from the back of her throat and it sounded like a protest. Because he'd kissed her or because he'd stopped? Regretfully, he set her gently back on the chair and her hands slid off his arms. She swallowed.

"Did that feel like a man who doesn't want you?" Zack was still bending over her, only an inch away from her face so his question was just above a whisper.

Skylar's long dark lashes fluttered open at the sound of his voice. She sucked her lower lip into her mouth, shaking her head.

He straightened and frowned down at her. "Okay, then. Romance it is, starting with dinner tomorrow night, just the two of us." He would sweep her off her feet, but at the end of it, he would have what he wanted. His ring on her finger and both of them winging their way back to New Zealand.

"But I warn you, I don't have time to play games. I need to be back home in New Zealand and I need you there with me."

He walked to the door, jiggling the lock a couple of times. It seemed to be working fine. "And just for the record—" he paused, waiting for her to look at him "—you got the sex perfectly right that night. Your only mistake was not locking the door."

Five

Nothing was going right! Skylar pouted at her reflection in the mirror. She couldn't find the butterfly clip of one of her only pair of earrings. There was barely a scrape of lip gloss left in the pot and the expensive perfume Eliza had given her for her twenty-first birthday wasn't her taste.

But the dress looked good. Better than good, she decided, turning this way and that in the big bathroom mirror.

Like the flesh of a russet apple, the rich color did something for her skin that made even her stupid freckles look okay. The split was indecent but worrying about that diluted her self-consciousness about the soft crepe fabric hugging her middle.

Personally she thought that looked beautiful. Seventeen weeks of pregnancy poked pridefully out against the dress, demanding attention.

And then her courage deserted her. Men liked flat tummies and big boobs, didn't they? The push-up strapless bra certainly enhanced her chest but she doubted Zack would even notice. All he'd see was that she appeared to have swallowed a small cantaloupe.

Why the heck hadn't she bought a tent to wear?

Close to tears by the time he knocked, she had a mind to turn out the lights and pretend not to be home. Darn pregnancy hormones. Darn Eliza, too, for being so far away. She could always rely on Eliza to make a silk purse out of a sow's ear.

Resigned, she picked up her shoes and the lovely raw silk wrap she had borrowed from Maya and tiptoed down the stairs. A full minute ticked by while she stood with her hand on the doorknob, squeezing her eyes shut to contain an unfamiliar panic.

Is this what you want, Zack Manning?

He'd raised his hand to knock again when she opened the door.

"I thought you'd—" his eyes moved from her face slowly down her body "—stood me up." He swallowed when his gaze reached her belly.

He was still staring when Skylar laughed nervously. "You have no idea how close I came." She moved aside and motioned him in.

Zack carried his jacket hooked in one finger over his shoulder. She tossed her shoes on the step and followed, thinking he did not look much like her stable hand tonight in dark pinstripes and a crisp white shirt. In fact, he was so handsome, she was reluctant to look at him out of fear that he'd see how much he affected her.

Zack turned at the fireplace and gave her another long look that seemed to soak through her skin and drug the flapping butterflies in her stomach. For a second, anyway.

"Wow!"

It sounded like "Whoa."

"You scrub up pretty well, Ms. Fortune."

Skylar twisted the wrap in her hands. "I'm a little worried." She looked down, grimacing. "About…" Her fingers fluttered in a nervous pass over her stomach.

His smile faded fast. "Worried?"

She warmed at his concern. "Not worried. Nervous." She took a quick breath and met his eyes. "I seem to have gained about a ton today."

Zack looked at her, his eyes crinkling at the corners. "You look…" he shook his head, as if he couldn't believe it "…amazing."

And suddenly, it was all right. The butterflies subsided and she realized how much she was looking forward to tonight. She *did* want to be seen with him, to sit in a fancy restaurant and have every women in the room envy her. To have his eyes focus on her all evening, ulterior motive and all. Just for tonight, Skylar wanted to try romance.

"Can I ask a favor?"

He looked at her expectantly.

"Can we just have, like, a first date? No talk of the future or weddings or even babies. Just two people trying to get to know each other."

Zack nodded. "We can." Then he pulled his jacket over his shoulder and reached into the inside pocket. "Almost forgot."

He drew out a long flat box covered in midnight blue velvet. Her heart stuttered. She'd never received a gift from a man before, unless you counted her family. She stepped forward shyly and their hands bumped as she shoved her wrap at him and took the box.

It was like nothing she had ever seen. Shades of sea-green and indigo and sunrise smoldered in front of her eyes. The colors of the necklace glowed like the shell of the mollusk depicted on a blurb pasted to the inside of the lid.

Skylar pursed her lips and breathed out the letter *P*.

"Paua. It's a species of abalone found down our way."

"And these are like pearls?"

Zack lifted the exquisite white gold chain. "A man-made particle is embedded by hand under the shell." He indicated she turn around. "Two or three years later, the pearl is harvested. The paua are farmed just for this process and like the real pearl, you don't always get a result."

His hand, roughened from his labors at the barn, brushed her hair from her nape, making her tingle. The three vertically set shimmering discs, interspersed with three small emerald-cut diamonds, nestled against her breastbone.

With his hands on her shoulders, he maneuvered her in front of the mirror above the fireplace. The person who stared back was a stranger. The necklace lent her a simple elegance she'd never possessed, complimented not only the structure of her neck but the texture of her skin and shape of her face.

Even more astonishing was Zack's face behind her, filled with pride and a hint of tender surprise, as if he'd been the one given an unexpected and cherished gift. They stared at each other for several moments before he bent and kissed her bare shoulder, a soft, lingering kiss that reassured and aroused at the same time.

Then he raised his head and looked at the necklace. "Uniquely New Zealand," he said softly, laying her wrap around her shoulders. "I had it made just for you."

She floated out to the car, feeling like Cinderella on her way to the ball. Her fingers hardly strayed from the beautiful necklace on the drive into town, loving the rich smoothness of it on her skin and fingertips.

They waited to be seated. This was not the most exclusive restaurant in town but it had built its reputation on romance and intimacy. It was dim and the tables were set around partitioning walls, bars and large potted plants, so once seated, the diners did not feel they were in a room full of other tables, because they were mostly hidden.

Zack's hand pressed on her lower back as they were led to their table but she checked at the sight of a familiar brown head.

"Creed!" The sole occupant of the table looked up, his mouth dropping open.

"Skylar." Creed half rose. "Wow. You look…"

Zack leaned toward him, hand outstretched.

"Hello, Zack. We haven't caught up." They shook hands.

Creed obviously hadn't been out to the estate since Zack's return.

"You have really come out of the closet," he commented with a pointed look at her midriff. "Are you sure it's wise to advertise?"

Skylar was busy checking out his table for signs of a companion. What was Creed doing in the most romantic restaurant in town, eating alone? "What do you want, to cram me into a girdle?"

"A little discretion goes a long way in this town when your surname happens to be Fortune." He paused, his eyes flicking from Skylar to Zack. "Unless of course you're about to announce your engagement."

You could always count on Creed and Case to have the best interests of the family reputation closest to their hearts. "You would have me locked up with my head shaved if you could," she retorted. "Talking of being discreet, what are you doing in this den of discretion? Is this where you bring your women?"

Creed gave a melancholy smile and glanced at the lone glass and solo setting.

She grinned. "Don't tell me you've been stood up?"

He shook his head. "I often eat here, alone or otherwise."

She immediately felt sorry and put her hand on his arm. "I guess it's not easy for you, seeing Sasha with Blake."

"Sasha and I were just friends and colleagues. She was helping me out."

They referred to his ex-employee who had accompanied Creed to public functions and social events for the last year or so, until Skylar's brother Blake swept her off her feet and they announced their engagement last month. Was Creed missing her? It was hard to tell. No one could accuse Creed of being lighthearted about anything.

"You'll find someone nice soon." The second the words were out of her mouth, she thought how patronizing and smug she sounded. Just because, for once in her life, she had *someone nice* take her out tonight and buy her precious jewelry.

Her guilt intensified when Creed looked positively glum. "Someone nice? I doubt that's possible."

Her curiosity bubbled up. Creed was often stern but she would not have described him as without hope.

"Don't worry about me," Creed said. "I'm just feeling a little sorry for myself." He gave her a wry grin. "Unrequited love is a terrible thing."

This was a night for surprises. Skylar's eyes widened and she opened her mouth but her half brother held up his hand. "And before you ask, no, I don't want to talk about it."

"Oh, but…"

Zack came to Creed's aid with an easy grin. "I'd ask you to join us, mate, but I'm working on that engagement you mentioned."

She forgot all about Creed and frowned at Zack. "You promised."

He nodded his head toward the maître d' who still hovered, waiting to see them to their table. "Shall we go eat?" he asked, an amused smile on his lips.

She turned back to Creed, who also looked amused. "I hate to see you sitting here, being miserable on your own."

"I'm not miserable. You run along." He turned to Zack. "The salmon is excellent here."

"What about the unrequited love?" She pouted. "Spill."

"Good night, Skylar. Zack. Enjoy your evening."

Zack tugged on her hand and she reluctantly moved off.

"Oh, and, Sky?"

She turned back.

"Pregnancy agrees with you. You look stunning."

Her mouth dropped open for a second. A compliment, from Creed. Almost unheard of. She let Zack lead her away, deep in thought.

They sat and ordered wine for Zack and a spiced tomato juice for Skylar. Her mind raced with possibilities
about her half brother's heartache. Who was the
mystery woman? It would be too terrible if it were
Sasha, despite his claims to the contrary.

"Hey, you." Zack's gently chiding voice brought her
eyes back to his face. "We're supposed to be having a
romantic dinner together, not wondering about your
brother's love life."

"Sorry." She smiled at him. "I've never wondered
about his love life in the past. He always seems so
distant."

He shrugged. "So the man has a heart."

"And it's hurting. Poor Creed. He makes out like
he's got it all together. Maybe I've misjudged him."

The drinks and menus arrived. Skylar was suddenly
ravenous and her mouth watered at the descriptions of
the dishes, although fine dining was nothing new for
someone brought up on the Fortune Estate. However,
sitting across a candlelit table from a man who set her
heart vibrating like wheels over a cattle guard, was a
unique experience. Her eyes flicked around the room.
There were probably thirty or forty people here but the
clever arrangement meant she could only see two tables
clearly. Both couples, both quite young. She wondered
if they were in love or breaking up, discussing business
or cheating on their wives.

"You grew up with Creed and Case, didn't you?"
Zack asked after the waiter finished taking their orders.

"And Eliza, yes."

"Why are you so distant?"

"Blake and I always felt like the poor cousins." She
played with the swizzle stick in her juice. "They never

forgave my mother for cheating on Dad. It was us against them." Her hand came up and fingered the lowest set pearl. "At least, it seemed that way when we were younger. I get on okay with them now in a sort of disconnected way. I know they're all concerned about me, as I am about them."

"My impression is they're all very fond of you. Now Blake, he's a different kettle of fish."

"Blake's always been confrontational. Especially after Dad handed the reins of the business to Case and Creed. He really felt that."

"He blames them?"

She nodded. "They offered him a place but he could never work under them. Still, he's done well for himself. I'm proud of him." She looked in the direction of her brother's table but could not see him. "I think Case and Creed are impressed by his achievements, too, even if they probably wouldn't say it."

As they ate, the talk mostly centered on horses and New Zealand. Zack kept his word and did not push her about weddings or the future. The meal was exquisite and Skylar reveled in his attention. She talked more about herself than she had ever done, due mostly to his skillful questioning.

"Have you always had a love affair with horses?"

"My father has always loved the track. He goes to all the big ones and the sales, too. My very first horse was a thoroughbred, Roscoe."

"Yet thoroughbreds are not that big here," Zack remarked.

"That's why it's such a thrill to have Black Power. Dad has a lot of contacts. He persuaded a big Kentucky breeder it would be a win-win situation to sell him to us for a fair price." She took a sip of water. "The breeder would get bragging rights and the industry would be better developed here. Nebraska and Minnesota are expanding their breeding and racing industries so they a good source of mares for me."

"And for Ace." He grinned.

After dessert, he sat back in his chair and just watched her for a minute or more without speaking. It was a measure of how comfortable Skylar felt that she did not mind his quiet study at all.

Finally, he spoke. "What gives, Skylar? Why is it that for the whole of the time I knew you until Case's wedding, you were this shy, stammering little thing who backed off whenever I looked at you and never dressed to impress—me or anyone?"

Dress to impress, one of her mother's mantras. High-impact impressions. That was Trina all over.

"Then the wedding," he continued. "You walked in with your head held high and made a beeline for me. We talked all night…danced." He raised his glass. "How do you do it? Go from one to the other?"

"Which do you prefer?" Her question was quiet but her heartbeat thumped in her ears.

"I can live with either," he replied seriously. "But it'll be a lot of fun guessing."

Max had once said his Kiwi friend was silver-tongued. Not in the smooth, glib, traditional sense, she decided, but he did often say exactly the right things.

"I blame you and Max for the night of the wedding." Skylar wrinkled her nose. "I liked you. I guess you knew that. Remember that day trip to my friend in Grand Island to see that stallion you were interested in shuttling? Max kept joshing me about not having a boyfriend to take to the wedding. Anyway, he said something crude and because you were there, I nearly died of embarrassment."

She glossed over it now but as much as she liked Max, she could have cheerfully throttled him that day.

"Freckles, you're too picky. Not surprising, given your occupation and proximity to the equine male reproductive organ. How can a mere man ever measure up?"

Skylar wouldn't have cared had Zack not been there. But given the infatuation that had gripped her by the throat over the last couple of weeks, her discomfort was intense. Through a haze of fire-engine red, she'd punched her cousin smartly on the arm, cursing him under her breath.

That wasn't the end of it.

"Then he said I had better watch out, that Eliza was after me to get all titivated up for the wedding."

"And I said—" Zack's eyes were bright with humor "—you wouldn't hold any truck with that rubbish, would you, Skylar? Fancy dresses, makeup, smelly perfume?"

She grimaced, recalling his muttered "give me horse sweat any day" comment.

"I was only trying to help," Zack insisted. "I could see you were embarrassed."

"Huh!"

"You stomped off then." He raised his eyes to the ceiling with an air of bafflement. "I said to Max I thought he'd offended you. He told me he thought what I'd said was much worse."

"Idiots, the pair of you," Skylar muttered.

That had been the catalyst. After a couple of weeks of wanting him to notice her. but feeling too shy to let him know, Skylar knew it was time to act or forever wonder. She was a twenty-four-year-old virgin. She had to sleep with someone, sometime. Why not the only man she had ever met who made her blood boil? "So, I thought, I'll show you. I can be grown-up and look good if I want to."

"So you let Eliza corner you."

"She's been trying most of my life to get me to look after my skin, cut my hair, get a manicure." Skylar smiled fondly. "I actually think Trina, my mother, had more of an influence on Eliza than she would own up to."

The best part of the whole plan was that he lived in New Zealand. Should Skylar miscalculate his interest or prove inferior in bed, then she didn't have to see him again. Her plan was perfect.

And to her surprise, things panned out so much better than she expected, until Maya's unfortunate interruption. For some reason, her brain functioned and she was able to conduct a conversation, even dance a step or two. For some reason, he seemed captivated by her. It was the best she had ever felt: knowing that she had turned his head, stole his breath, transfixed him for a few short hours.

He was as frantic with lust as she when they sneaked away from the post-wedding party at the big house and she dragged him upstairs to her bedroom. Their lovemaking would live on in her memory forever. Intense, four-hundred times more exciting than anything she had ever experienced and mind-numbingly satisfying.

Skylar looked down at her tummy. There was no way in the world she could have foreseen these consequences that night. What was it about getting dressed up that lent her confidence and poise and made her interesting to the opposite sex? A pretty dress was like a magic cloak, borrowed for a sliver of time. No doubt tomorrow, she would appear as tongue-tied, boring and scruffy as usual.

"I suppose I threw myself at you," she said wryly.

Zack shook his head. "You didn't have to. I came running." The smile faded. "And I didn't protect you that night. I feel bad about that."

She sighed, rubbing her bare arms. "It's not how I thought things would turn out. I wanted you to show me what it was all about, that's all."

"But you didn't want anything to do with me afterward."

"I did," she insisted. "I was ashamed. I wanted to believe I could carry off this cool, sophisticated rendezvous." She smiled down at her glass. "Instead, I ended up making a big mess of things."

Zack reached for her hand with both of his. Surprise and anticipation shivered through her, intensifying when she felt his feet under the table sandwich both of hers between them.

"Uh-uh." He shook his head. "I wouldn't have missed that for the world."

That rocked her. Part of her, a big part, fell in love with him right then. Even so, she worried she'd be burned. If he only knew that, should he mention marriage at this very minute, Skylar would probably clamber right over the tabletop to acquiesce.

The whisper-light touch of his fingers on her upturned palm sent a lick of excitement shooting up her arm. He shifted closer to the table and darned if she didn't, too, so that one of her knees was firmly trapped between both of his.

Zack laced his fingers with hers. "Why did you leave it so long to tell me?"

"I was a coward," she murmured, and looked away but her fingers squeezed his gently. "I've never been good with words and this was the biggest thing that ever happened to me. I wanted to keep it safe…I don't know. But I really was going to call you the night you arrived."

His thumb stroked along the inside of her wrist and their eyes met. He believed her, she could see that, even through the dizzying array of emotion and fear and rising excitement. His touch branded her and she shivered, wanting more.

Suddenly, everything seemed shiny and new. The flowers and candles on the table. The muted voices and low musical tones of some hidden stereo…the respect of the waiters. The man sitting opposite her with his sharp, wanting eyes. This was the stuff of her dreams since the moment Max introduced them. Would he clasp her hand and tell her quietly that he loved her?

The waiter slid her cup of decaf in front of her and she reluctantly pulled her hand from his, before she dissolved into fantasyland. "How did you and Max get together, anyway?"

Skylar knew her cousin and Zack were business partners but that was about it.

"We played rugby for university in Sydney," he replied, stirring his coffee. "Went traveling for a bit. When we came home, we pooled our resources…" He chuckled. "Mostly Max's resources, I would have to say, and set up a backpackers' bus company. It went off like a rocket. Pretty soon, there were thirty buses wandering around the country with our logo on them. It made sense to expand into New Zealand since most back-packers would travel both countries if they were going that far."

She frowned. "I'm confused. Are you a New Zealander or an Australian?"

Zack paused, monitoring his thoughts. There was a limit to the amount of information he wanted to divulge at this point. "I grew up in Australia but my mother was a Kiwi and New Zealand feels like home now. I spent a couple of months setting up the bus company there and then we discovered franchises. It looked like a good opportunity to make a killing for half the work."

Both had been amazed at the roll of successes they accumulated in a very short time. With Max's sharp eye for a bargain and seemingly unlimited resources and Zack's cutthroat instincts toward marketing and economic trends, the pair were soon ensconced as a parent company of twenty or thirty different franchise companies. They moved into the lucrative arena of the stock market. By then, they were household names.

Zack had, for a while, enjoyed the cut and thrust of business and gambling on the market. In all, they had spent less than a decade setting up an explosion of small home-based franchises that needed little guidance. There was a head office in Sydney and another office in Auckland.

Then Max wanted to take on more responsibility at his ranch and Zack suddenly found himself with a very good reason to tire of the publicity their risky and entrepreneurial exploits attracted.

But he wouldn't go into that right now.

"I needed another challenge," he told her. "So I

moved down south and bought a winery, one that was just starting out and needed some decent marketing to make it fly."

"And the name Greta?"

Greta Wines and now Greta Stud were now the most important things in Zack's life, along with the woman and the baby she carried sitting across the table from him. "It was my mother's name." His mother's real name, as he found out when she died after a long battle with cancer.

Gill Manning was really Greta Thorne. All his life, she had adamantly refused to talk of his father, saying he was either in prison or dead. She told him he must never try to find out about him or great harm would come to both of them. Zack believed she really was afraid because they packed up and moved on every year or so. As he grew old enough and then rich enough to find out for himself, she made him promise to leave it alone. Only harm would come to both of them if he meddled in the past, she said. Later, when she fell ill, he didn't have the heart to go against her wishes.

But the day she died, his responsibility for her died, too. He needed to know. So he hired a private investigator to map out her life.

It was a shock to find his mother's family was *the* prominent family in New Zealand politics. There were two former prime ministers, and even now, his mother's oldest brother was the leader of the main opposition party.

But his reception with that esteemed family was anything but warm. They turned their backs, saying Greta had died for them the day she ran off to Australia.

"I thought it might be a girlfriend's name." Skylar folded her arms and leaned on the table, her eyes down.

Zack watched her chew on her bottom lip. The perfect out to change a subject he needed to keep under wraps for now. He lowered his head so he could see under her downcast face, encouraging her to look at him. "If you want to know, just ask," he told her, amused.

She looked into the flame of the candle and raised her shoulders.

"I was seeing a woman in Australia every month or so for a couple of years, but it was a very casual, open-ended thing. It suited both of us that way."

He had to strain to hear her question. "Was?"

"I finished it." He paused, then added, "The other day."

The flame of the candle wavered drunkenly with her exhalation but still she did not look at him. "Was she upset?"

"Not overly. We'll probably remain friends. I always seem to stay friends."

"What was she like? Pretty, I bet."

"Well, she didn't have your cute smile," he teased. "No freckles, poor thing, and her eyes were kind of muddy looking. Not like your baby blues."

She smiled and rested her flushed cheek in one hand. "You're making fun."

"Maybe." He was discovering he liked making her blush.

"So you bought the vineyard. Why the stud? They don't exactly go together."

"Max's idea. Over a few beers last year at the Melbourne Cup, we decided it would be fun to breed a winner."

Her brows furrowed. "You must be rich if you can afford to throw millions at a bit of fun."

"I do all right," he told her. "If that's what's worrying you."

Her lips curved a fraction. "We nearly made it through dinner."

Zack stroked his chin, wondering what it was about her smile that pulled at him. She was pretty, quite beautiful tonight, but nice dinners with lovely women weren't new for him. Forging closer personal ties was, and sometimes she made it difficult for him to remember that he was here for one purpose only—to secure a part in his son's or daughter's life and make up for all the years of being denied a family.

Sometimes she also made it difficult to remember when he'd ever wanted someone so badly… "But will we make it home before I kiss you?"

The drop of her necklace rippled as Skylar swallowed. She had no answer to that. Zack crossed his ankles around hers, trapping her again. She looked away but he saw the tremble in her fingers as she picked up and drained her coffee cup. When her other leg pressed tentatively against his a few seconds later, he could not help his satisfied smile.

Zack signaled the waiter for the check. He brushed her arms, settling her wrap around her shoulders and held her hand while they waited for the car to be brought around. As he leaned over her to open the door, their eyes met and held. Skylar finally broke the connection, by looking down at his mouth. Zack tipped her chin up with his index finger, employing his other hand to caress her skin under the foam of silk around her shoulders.

She was perfectly still, her arms by her sides, her lips slightly parted. Zack moved his bottom lip over the seam of her mouth until she raised her eyes to him. "I guess not..." he whispered. She did not move back and so he took her mouth, watching until her eyelids fluttered down.

He pressed her closer, kissing her deeply. Her hair was silky between his fingers. This wasn't just a taste now. Her night of romance, all wrapped up and tied with a bow. He used all his so-called expertise to show his desire and stoke hers.

But the joke was on him. Suddenly, he was starving for her, as if he hadn't just spent a couple hundred dollars on food. It was her mouth and skin he wanted and he feasted until the moment when he felt her knees began to buckle. Only then did he pull back and let her slide into the car.

Six

Barely breathing, she held herself still so she could not feel anything but the memory of his mouth on hers, his warm hand caressing her shoulder and pressing on her back, his fingers combing through her hair.

She had so little to compare his kisses to. A couple of uncomfortable fumbles at college and then that magical night a few months ago.

But tonight his kiss was quite different to the fire and passion he had overwhelmed her with before. Back then, he'd given her no room to move, no time to think. And that was just the way she wanted it. Tonight, he was much more measured—a planned seduction.

And again, that was just the way she wanted it.

His mouth had just the perfect touch of firm and a hint of need. The spread-out hand on her back suggested control and his fingers used her hair so gently to coax her head back to just the right angle to be kissed.

His kisses were intoxicating. How could she resist? And why would she want to?

Because time did not seem to register, it jolted her to hear the crunch of the estate's gravel driveway in her ears. Even louder was the silence when he rolled to a halt.

He'd turned the engine off. She had a decision to make.

And in her mind, Skylar had probably made the decision when he gave her the necklace.

So she took her keys from her purse and offered them to him, still staring straight ahead. "Because—I don't know how to say—" she faltered, feeling his eyes on her "—what I want…"

Seconds dragged by. She held out the keys like she was passing the salt. Wouldn't it be hysterical if he turned her down?

Finally, finally, she felt his warm hand on hers.

"Loud and clear," Zack said in a gruff voice and took the keys from her fingers. He got out of the car and she followed, waiting in an agony of nerves while he unlocked the door. She moved forward into the darkened hallway and heard the sharp double click of the door being closed and locked.

And then she felt his hands on her arms, his lips brushing her ear from behind.

"Can you—can you take the necklace off?" she whispered. "I don't want to break it."

His hands stroked up her arms and she shivered. She felt him release the catch and the slow slide of the chain and then his mouth on the top of her shoulder, chasing down her butterflies, whipping them into a frenzy.

Zack turned her gently to face him. His hand came up and cupped her face. "Nervous?"

Skylar nodded, swallowing hard.

"More than the first time?"

"Yes." She gulped, berating herself. It was a bit late to play the blushing virgin now. But four months ago, she'd had a couple of glasses of wine and several dances pressed up against his body. The knowledge that he'd be leaving in the morning. She was so eager, she'd practically torn his clothes off.

But this was another night. He bent his head. "Kiss me." He tapped the corner of his mouth with his index finger. "Here."

Skylar hesitated then rose up onto her toes and dusted a closed-mouth kiss where his finger had been. He smelled sexy and expensive and all male.

"Sweet." He slid one arm around her waist. "And here." He tapped the other corner of his mouth, his chin raised expectantly.

She did as he asked, recognizing that he was allowing her to set the pace. Emboldened, she raised her hands and caged his face, kissing him squarely on the mouth and lingering now. Parting her lips just a little. Tasting and breathing him in.

And suddenly, the nerves slid away and she felt comfortable enough to explore and indulge her curiosity. Her hands snaked around his neck and played with his hair, combing her fingers through. She kissed him a little harder then tried fisting her hands in his hair and tugging his head down with the slightest of pressure.

He slid his other arm around her waist and, still with her mouth locked on his, she pressed up against him, sighing with pleasure. And it was a pleasure. With her arms up around his neck, her whole body melded the length of his, soft curves against lean, tight muscle. His legs braced firmly as she leaned into him, her bulge between them the only scrap of distance.

The kisses deepened and her excitement grew. His tongue probed and now there was nothing tentative about her response. The thrill made her feel like a billion champagne bubbles, steeped in exhilaration. By the time he dragged his mouth off hers and backed up, leading her to the bottom of her stairs, Skylar had to force herself not to race him, just as she had that first night.

The bedroom was dark but she stayed his hand from the light switch. Zack took both ends of the wrap and slid it sideways, back and forth over her back and shoulders. The sensuous feel of the cool silk on her hot flesh warmed her and she arched, her tummy bumping him. To steady herself, she put her hands around his neck again and he moved forward and took her mouth.

The one or two times she had tried openmouthed kissing had been unmemorable, even distasteful. Not with Zack. Now she yearned to be invaded, to taste and test the texture of him on her tongue. She sank into his hot mouth and plunged her hands into his hair. His hands stroked down her sides and then up her back and he pressed her in. Her soft curves melted against his hard and tightly muscled form. She gasped at the feel of his erection rubbing just above her pubic bone at the swell of her tummy. She wanted more. Wanted everything. Her whole body tingled with impatience.

His hands found her zipper, which ran from the middle of her back down to the provocative split of the dress. In the back of her mind, she felt the zipper coming down, the fabric loosening. But when the fabric whispered over the tips of her breasts and kept moving southward, she stiffened and clamped one arm around the top of her abdomen, halting its progress.

She didn't want him to see her. Over his shoulder the light from the hall spilled into the room through the open door.

She could still see his features, the blaze of desire, the questioning look. But she didn't want to see his face when he finally saw her naked. Yes, he had made her feel beautiful tonight with his gift and his wanting eyes. But this was down to the nitty-gritty now. "You won't—you won't be shocked at my big belly, will you?"

His mouth turned up. He leaned forward and nuzzled her neck. "I'm looking forward to introducing myself." He nibbled kisses on her throat and at the base of her ear and she tried so hard to rise to the same heart pounding excitement again and nearly succeeded. Until he unfastened her bra. She flinched. Her breasts quivered at the withdrawal of support.

Zack leaned back and looked at her again, concern in his eyes. "Are your breasts sore?"

"Sensitive."

His kisses glided down her throat, while his hands supported and lifted her breasts. His fingers rubbed and squeezed and she arched her spine, needing more, needing something else and finally she felt first his palms and then his fingers circle her nipples, touching every tiny bump in her engorged areolae like Braille.

He knew just what to do to blow her mind. Cupping her firmly, he licked first one then the other aching tip, blowing on them and the chilly air was torture. With relief she saw his head move forward and he took one large dark nipple into his mouth. She gulped and pushed forward insistently, inciting him to suck. The pleasure was exquisite, one click short of pain and she wondered if she was supposed to want this so much when she was a few short months away from having her baby suckle her.

But this distraction couldn't stop her clamping her arm against the dress when his hands began smoothing it down again. Instantly Zack pulled back. "Still nervous?"

What he must think of her! "It's just—" she ducked her head, knowing he could see her embarrassment "—It's big, bigger than you think. And the belly button looks funny, not out, just flat. And there's this weird line down the middle that goes right from my belly button to my…"

"Linea negra," he murmured.

"No, to my…" And then her face burned with embarrassment as his words sank in.

Stupid to think he wouldn't have read up on every stage of her pregnancy.

Zack tilted her chin up and brushed her lips with his mouth. "Sky, nothing is going to happen that you don't want."

He thought she didn't want him? "Oh, but I do want. I do. Only, can we close the door? Do it in the dark?"

If he was disappointed, he didn't show it. "The first time, then." He released her and closed the door then drew her close and kissed her tenderly. "Do you have any idea how beautiful you are to me?" He tapped her nose with his index finger and she opened her eyes. "All of you." As he spoke, he ran his hands up her spine.

She inhaled, weak with relief that now he was just a

dark outline and she couldn't make out his features. Her overriding desire now was to touch him, all of him. So she set about undressing him. But it proved tough to undo buttons one handed so she had to let the dress go.

Her eyes closed with deep sensuous pleasure as she skimmed over the skin of his chest and shoulders and arms. The shape of him flowed into her fingertips, like a piece of music or a great film, taking her where she wanted to go. A little scared, a lot curious and overwhelmingly excited, she breathed a sigh of relief when she managed to get his zipper down without mangling him.

He leaned into her. Overcome by the unfamiliarity of her skin pressing against his, she swayed a little. "You okay?"

She nodded and put her hands on his hips and they kissed, deep and carnal. Soft against hard, her blood pounded as he moved his mouth down her body, inch by inch. Insecurities faded away as an erotic charge flooded her senses. She swayed and squirmed and pleaded for more as his hands stroked over every inch of her. Through a rapidly building haze of excitement, she felt the slow slide of her panties down her legs, legs that were being coaxed apart by a thousand nibbling kisses and his thumbs pressing purposefully up her inner thighs.

She came apart at the very first touch, but Zack showed no mercy. He licked and sucked until her body stopped cramping, the initial white-hot blast washed by a wave of ecstasy that slowly ebbed away.

Her knees buckled when he took his mouth away, as if that was the only thing holding her up.

"I've got you," he murmured, pulling her close.

Boneless, she sagged against him, curling her toes at the aftershocks that continued to ripple through her.

Zack turned his head and licked the corner of her lips. She opened to him and they kissed deeply, his need giving an edge to her satisfaction and leaving her wanting, too. Like chocolate, she couldn't get enough.

He pushed against her and she jolted as that hot, velvety length slid against flesh still absorbing and throbbing with prickles of intense pleasure. She gripped him between her legs and moved back and forth, slick and burning. He grunted and backed up toward the bed, pulling her down on top of him.

This was completely new for her but somehow it all seemed so natural. A natural progression from feeling so vulnerable about her nudity to standing while he pleasured her intimately to now levering herself above him, torturing him with slow teasing slides of her body over his. She found the power to tease was its own aphrodisiac.

But her own excitement was her undoing. Bold now, she teased him just an inch too far, a slight and mostly unintentional miscalculation. She'd known he was quick and she could, in all honesty, have reneged on the deal, but the sensation of him slipping just inside and the anticipation of lots of hot, hard flesh filling her, was irresistible.

Skylar eased down, slowly at first, adjusting to the fiery heat. She began to rock, raising up a little, changing angles to build and prolong the pleasure coursing through her. His hands firmed on her hips and he moved inside her with a delicious friction, molten with a centre of steel. Tension built quickly and warmth flooded her body and mind. And when Zack felt her tremors begin he thrust up strongly, pulling her hips down and she tumbled into an ecstasy that was relentless and mind shattering in its power.

* * *

Zack opened his eyes when he felt her face bury into his shoulder. He huffed in a gathering breath and turned to look at her—what he could see of her. A curtain of light caramel hair covered most of her face, along with his shoulder, but a little patch of creased forehead told of her screwed up eyes.

She wasn't going to block him out again. Zack did not sleep with women he didn't like. Just as important as arousal was the aftermath. It bothered him that bonding with Skylar after their first time had not been an option. That was not going to happen tonight, especially with so much riding on it.

"Hey, you." He blew on her hair, sending a section rising sharply and then flopping down. "Wake up."

She screwed her face up harder and rubbed her nose on his skin. "Not asleep."

Zack eased over onto his side so he was facing her. "Don't you go all shy on me again." Reaching out, he brushed the hair off her face. "Wasn't so bad, was it?"

An expulsion of air escaped her nostrils and she shook her head. He leaned toward her and dropped a kiss on her nose.

"Was it—different?" she asked, finally looking at him. "With the bulge and all?"

Too right, it was. An amazing, magical feeling making love to a woman growing big with his child—either that, or the lack of a rubber, a rare occurrence over the years.

"Different? Yeah, it was special." He brought his hand down between them and laid it on her belly, feeling a rush of emotion. "More of a connection because of what's in here."

That's what he'd missed since Rhianne, the tenderness. And it wasn't just tonight, because of the baby lying between them. Their first night together had also given him that feeling, though he'd supposed at the time that was because he'd been her first. Virginity was a gift and carried responsibility, in Zack's mind.

"But physically?"

"Physically, it was great. What's worrying you?"

"Just that, because of the baby, you feel you have to be gentle. Would you normally be gentle?"

Zack considered. "There's a place for gentleness, just like there's a place for fun and intensity and sometimes just out-and-out hot sex." He tilted her face up to his and brushed her lips with his own. "It's all good, Skylar, as long as you're both on the same wavelength at the same time."

She squirmed a little under his gaze. "But what if, when I'm not pregnant anymore, you don't feel the same connection?"

Zack smiled at her reference to a future for them. At least she was entertaining the thought. "I already had the connection. I have had for months."

Her mouth twisted. "Really?"

Zack bristled at the note of skepticism in her tone. "I don't make promises I won't keep, Skylar. I wanted you before, I want you now, and I see no reason not to keep wanting you."

She looked away, but he gripped her chin firmly, forcing her to look back.

"Where does this insecurity, this lack of self-esteem come from?"

No response, which was going to get her exactly nowhere, Zack decided. "You're pretty, you're intelligent.

You're successful at what you do and have a fantastic rep in breeding circles. Why is it so hard to believe someone could want you?"

"I believe what you want is this." She cast her eyes downward, to where his hand still rested on her stomach.

He frowned. "I do. Very much. Listen, I know you'll be an amazing mother. I know that this baby will have a great life and not want for anything. But you're nuts if you think I would marry you if I didn't want to be with you. If I didn't think we were a good fit."

It was dark in the room but Zack thought he saw her eyes light up with hope. In the silence that followed, he castigated himself for turning the aftermath of lovemaking into another demand. He had intended to keep his promise not to talk about the future or the baby. This was supposed to be her night, her one perfect night. The gift, the meal, the lovemaking—he could afford one night.

"One thing about pregnancy," she murmured, pushing away from him. "The pressure on your bladder. S'cuse me."

Zack turned a bedside lamp on, plumped up the pillows and lounged back with his hands behind his head. Surprised, he realized he hadn't noticed last time how feminine her room was. She gave the impression she didn't give a damn about her sexuality but her room was nice. Tasteful, elegant, understated. Come to think of it, the furniture and decor downstairs were elegant and comfortable, too.

Skylar returned, rubbing her hands together and making a Scottish laird proud with her rendition of *brr*. He made a tent with the covers and she clambered in and snuggled up, shivering with theatrical comedy.

"I like your room." He rested his chin on her head and inhaled a fresh burst of toothpaste. "Not what I expected."

"Too girly, you mean. Eliza helped. She loves decorating."

"You make out that you're not girly," he teased, "but I sense a latent femininity."

"Maya says I wear my clothes like a shield," she mused, spreading her fingers on his chest.

"They do shout 'back off!'" he agreed. "Why is that?"

Skylar sniffed. "Dunno. I wasn't without role models. Eliza." She paused. "My mother."

Zack was curious about her mother. "I met her once when Max and I spent a night at Blake's casino in Deadwood. She's a beautiful woman." *Beautiful but shallow. Brittle temperment, calculating mind.*

"Did she come on to you?" Skylar raised up, a suspicious twist to her mouth.

"No. She was preoccupied." With a white-haired high roller, Zack recalled. Older, exuding wealth and flashy gold on his fingers and wrist.

"Humph." She subsided, nestling back down and put a tentative hand on his chest. "She usually is."

It sounded like Skylar did not wholly approve of her mother. Maybe that's why she dressed the way she did, to avoid the comparisons. Because there were comparisons. High cheekbones, creamy skin, the sweep of a wide, shapely mouth. But Skylar was taller, more solid, more earthy and real. "Don't you get on?" He covered her hand with his and began to move it in slow circles on his skin, encouraging her to feel.

"I'm a disappointment. Not glamorous or sophisticated."

The Silhouette Reader Service™ — Here's how it works:

Accepting your 2 free books and 2 free mystery gifts places you under no obligation to buy anything. You may keep the books and gifts and return the shipping statement marked "cancel". If you do not cancel, about a month later we'll send you 6 additional books and bill you just $3.80 each in the U.S. or $4.47 each in Canada, plus 25¢ shipping & handling per book and applicable taxes if any.* That's the complete price and — compared to cover prices of $4.50 each in the U.S. and $5.25 each in Canada — it's quite a bargain! You may cancel at any time, but if you choose to continue, every month we'll send you 6 more books, which you may either purchase at the discount price or return to us and cancel your subscription.

*Terms and prices subject to change without notice. Sales tax applicable in N.Y. Canadian residents will be charged applicable provincial taxes and GST. All orders subject to approval. Credit or debit balances in a customer's account(s) may be offset by any other outstanding balance owed by or to the customer. Please allow 4 to 6 weeks for delivery.

If offer card is missing write to: Silhouette Reader Service, 3010 Walden Ave., P.O. Box 1867, Buffalo NY 14240-1867

NO POSTAGE
NECESSARY
IF MAILED
IN THE
UNITED STATES

BUSINESS REPLY MAIL
FIRST-CLASS MAIL   PERMIT NO. 717   BUFFALO, NY

POSTAGE WILL BE PAID BY ADDRESSEE

SILHOUETTE READER SERVICE
3010 WALDEN AVE
PO BOX 1867
BUFFALO NY 14240-9952

GET FREE BOOKS and FREE GIFTS WHEN YOU PLAY THE...

SLOT MACHINE GAME!

Just scratch off the silver box with a coin. Then check below to see the gifts you get!

YES!

I have scratched off the silver box. Please send me the 2 free Silhouette Desire® books and 2 free gifts for which I qualify. I understand I am under no obligation to purchase any books, as explained on the back of this card.

326 SDL ELYM   225 SDL ELQA

FIRST NAME	LAST NAME

ADDRESS

APT.#	CITY

STATE/PROV.	ZIP/POSTAL CODE

7	7	7	**Worth TWO FREE BOOKS plus 2 BONUS Mystery Gifts!**
🍒	🍒	🍒	**Worth TWO FREE BOOKS!**
♣	♣	♣	**Worth ONE FREE BOOK!**
🔔	🔔	🍒	**TRY AGAIN!**

www.eHarlequin.com

(S-D-05/07)

Offer limited to one per household and not valid to current Silhouette Desire® subscribers.

Your Privacy - Silhouette Books is committed to protecting your privacy. Our Privacy Policy is available online at www.eHarlequin.com or upon request from the Silhouette Reader Service. From time to time we make our lists of customers available to reputable firms who may have a product or service of interest to you. If you would prefer for us not to share your name and address, please check here ☐

He smiled at the small hitch in her breath and the resistance in her wrist when he directed her fingers over his nipples.

"I don't go out with any of the guys she tries to hook me up with."

No, from what he'd observed, Skylar would definitely not be interested in the crowd her mother ran with. *Thank God.*

Under his hand, her fingers curled as the tips circled lightly over his nipples. Little tingles of awareness chased his interest in her mother away. He eased their hands over his chest and abdomen moving from side to side in a slow exploration.

"Zack?"

"Mmm?" The slow dance on his skin was lighting fires everywhere. Her head was still on his shoulder, looking down but he was covered by the sheet.

"I'm curious."

"Curious is good." He rubbed his chin up and down in her hair. Tracked the enthralling journey of their hands down to where he felt most powerful, yet willing to beg.

"I've never seen—or touched—a naked man before. Not really."

He sucked in his stomach as their hands continued lower.

"That's a terrible shortcoming," he murmured into her hair. "Let's remedy that."

It seemed no time at all until the alarm buzzed in his ears. Zack woke with a bursting bladder and an equally insistent erection. *Down, boy!* In her condition she needed her sleep. They'd had precious little in the night, where Zack found, to his delight, that lying with a curious and inexperienced woman had its advantages.

Skylar could be in no doubt now about how well they were suited. The whole evening was a resounding success and moved him that much closer to his goal. And it had been no hardship at all.

"We were lucky with the alarms," Skylar mumbled, allowing herself a catlike stretch.

She was referring to the foaling alarms. Because of the lateness of the breeding season, the pager had only sounded once, and when Skylar called in, Bob told her he could handle things.

"Up and at 'em." He groaned then leaned forward to nip her shoulder. "As my mother used to say."

She snuggled even deeper under the covers while he dragged himself out of the bed. "Did your parents divorce, Zack?"

He tensed. "Why do you ask?"

A hand escaped the covers and she rubbed at her nose. He relaxed a little, seeing she was seconds away from falling back to sleep. Idle curiosity, that's all. He bent and scooped up his suit trousers, grimacing when he realized he would have to make the walk to his room in the big house to change.

"You always say 'my mother,' 'my father.' Never 'my parents.'"

Zack zipped up his pants and sat on the edge of the bed to drag on socks. "Your parents are divorced," he reminded her. "What our parents did has no bearing on us. I for one, don't believe in divorce."

He turned to look at her. Only her face showed above the covers. "Wouldn't it make sense, Skylar, for me to come and go to the stables from here?"

She kept her eyes closed but he noted the swallow and the almost imperceptible shake of her head.

Not yet. She didn't trust him yet.

Disappointment dampened his earlier smug cheer. He got up and shrugged into his shirt. So there was a bit more work to do yet.

He took a last look at the sexy, tousled woman in the bed. "It's a poor show," he told her, "when a man has to sneak into his lover's parent's house to find his pants."

Her delectable mouth curved in a wicked smile. "Want me to come and hold your hand?"

"Stay." He leaned forward and kissed the smile away.

Seven

Later in the afternoon, she sneaked into the breeding shed to watch Ace at work. The teaser had been and gone and the mare stood quietly awaiting the arrival of Black Power. She was a pretty thing, even with the twitch on her upper lip and padded booties on her hind legs to minimize any damage she may try to inflict on her beau.

Oh, he was beautiful, she thought as Bob led him in, sleek and high stepping through the woodchips carpeting the floor. Even at this late stage of the breeding season, he was the total professional. Led to the mare, he introduced himself, nuzzling her neck and shoulders, moving down her body with lips turned in and nibbling gently. It was brief and fairly unimaginative as foreplay went but seemed to have the desired effect on both parties.

Once Ace got down to business though, the tenderness was out the window as he carried out his duty with his teeth embedded in the mare's neck.

She watched proudly as her team moved unhurriedly around the breeding shed, carrying out their appointed tasks. All of them except for young Ben had worked at Fortune Stud since Skylar started and they were a pretty efficient and well-oiled team.

The owner was from New York City, although his mare boarded in South Dakota close to Rapid City. He was new to the breeding game and had made the trip especially to see Black Power at work. "Is it always so quick and brutal?" he asked, wide-eyed, as the stud heaved himself off the mare's back.

"Every stud is different," Skylar told him. "Demetrius, my other stallion, is more your *wham bam thank you, ma'am,* sort of guy, but he's nicer than Ace at the finish. He'll always rest his neck on hers for a few seconds afterward."

Zack, who'd been given the job of soothing and distracting the mare, chose that moment to give her a long slow look that made her giddy. So giddy that she wasn't watching when Ben, charged with washing the stallion down, inexplicably kept the handheld shower nozzle pointed up as Bob led Ace away, soaking the hindquarters of the mare and the astonished owner. Despite Skylar's and the white-faced boy's repeated apologies, the man turned decidedly frosty and stomped off to his horse van, brushing at his expensive damp suit.

Skylar was peeved at Ben's lack of concentration. A lot of her business was word-of-mouth. There could be expensive consequences if the disgruntled breeder from

New York put the word around. At least Black Power had performed with his usual consummate professionalism.

Later she walked home and took a shower, changing into a long peasant skirt and one of her new long-sleeved T-shirts. When she'd left, Zack was busy loading the mare back into her van and setting up for Deme's cover. He hadn't said when or if he would come again and Skylar was too shy to ask in front of the men.

She was studying the meager contents of her fridge, thankful she hadn't invited him for dinner when he knocked. He'd come straight from the stables, still dusty, his clothes streaked with horse sweat and peppered with flakes of sweetfeed. The moment the door closed behind him, he dragged her into his arms and kissed her until she was breathless.

"I've been thinking about this all day," he growled, propelling her toward the stairs. She gasped at the feel of his rough hands on her skin as they slipped under her top. The smell of sweat and grain and horse fed her need. She loved that she was clean and fragrant and he wasn't, but now wasn't the time to analyze her weird appetites. Now was the time to celebrate and indulge them.

Mouths locked, they crab-walked up the stairs, both sets of hands fumbling with buttons and zippers. Their clothing littered the short corridor to her room, forlorn shapeless shirts with noodle arms, her bra still fastened, dragged over her head and hanging drunkenly by one strap from the doorknob. Zack hopped on one leg to the bed, battling jeans that had snagged on his shoes. Noses, teeth, foreheads, elbows all bumped to the music of labored breaths and the odd giggle from Skylar.

Finally they were naked, stretched out against each other on the bed and Skylar thought her heart would explode out of her chest. So this was his idea of out-and-out hot sex. Edgy, desperate, irresponsible when she thought fleetingly of the unlocked door downstairs.

But one thing she found, when he snagged her wrists with the fingers of one hand and loomed over her, was that trust beat in the roaring of her blood. He filled her in one long restrained slide, careful to keep his weight off her body. And then he rolled so she lay on top and she drew her knees up until she straddled him and began to move.

"I have no idea what I'm doing," she whispered, her legs scissored around his waist. She drowned in a desire she had never dreamed of and then a wash of pleasure that was impossible in its intensity. He felt beautiful moving inside her—she felt beautiful draped around him. She pulled away from his mouth and sat up, un-caring about her bulge of a tummy, all self-conscious-ness gone. He made her feel beautiful.

But when she felt the tremors start and swell and crash over her, her body collapsed down onto him and his rigid flesh and strong hands gripping her hips were the only things that kept her from shattering.

A couple of hours later they finally made it down-stairs to eat. Skylar pulled her hair back in a damp pony-tail as they walked down the stairs. Zack smelled a whole lot better after their bath but unfortunately had to don the same clothes he'd arrived in.

Skylar heeded this and tried to figure out an opening to say she had a spare key should he feel like going to his room in the big house and bringing a few things back for the morning. But out of a pretty dress, or out of bed, it seemed she would always be dogged by shyness.

They ate grilled cheese sandwiches in front of the gas fire. Zack put his empty plate aside, pulled her down in front of him on the sofa and wrapped his arms around her middle. "Do you see how good we are together?"

His breath tickled her ear. "Mmm." Her skin tingled in remembrance. "If I'd known how good it could feel, I wouldn't have waited so long."

Even without seeing his face, she felt the change in his mood, the leap from lazy fulfillment to steely determination.

"It could be like this every day," he told her, his voice deceptively soft.

"Could it?" Her eyes flicked around the room while she struggled to formulate a reply. "I feel like we're just getting started."

Zack exhaled and slipped his hands under her T-shirt, cupping her bulge. "Skylar, I've missed enough of this pregnancy. I want to be there every step of the way from here on in."

His meaning was clear: she should have told him earlier. But she so loved the newness of this, the novelty of having someone desire her. He was asking her to leap from excitement and passion straight into marriage. Would the fire they seemed to ignite in each other fade once he had what he wanted?

"I just wish it wasn't so far away," she hedged, staring at the blank TV screen.

"You will like it there, I promise." He covered her hand with both of his. "What are you scared of?"

Being stranded in a strange country when you decide you don't want me anymore. "I don't even know what the law is. We could split up and maybe I won't be allowed to bring the baby home."

"Wouldn't you rather consider the probability that we'll be very happy together?"

He had no idea how much she wanted that and if another life wasn't involved, she might risk it. "I'd rather consider that probability when I've had a bit more time to get used to the idea."

Zack stopped rubbing her tummy. "You know what my situation is. I have two new businesses, which I'm still learning about, and I can't do that from here. Once they're fully up and running and I've got the marketing on track, I can be more flexible. What I don't want is to be going backward and forward every other week while you make up your mind." He shifted behind her. "You owe me, Skylar, the next few months. Don't deny me the chance to watch you growing big with our child."

She leaned back into him until she felt his cheek on hers. It was very tempting. Her infatuation was so much more advanced. She forced her mind to consider the possibility of him leaving her now.

It left a black hole of despair.

Skylar knew it was impossible to have exactly what she wanted—Zack living here with her and her baby. He was a man. She was supposed to want to follow. Women always had to make the sacrifices.

But it was asking a heck of a lot to give up her safety net. "Who runs my place in the meantime?" Somehow she knew he would have an answer for that, too.

He did. "There are management agencies for that sort of thing, or you could promote Bob. He's managed bigger operations than this before."

Her pager bleeped. Relieved, Skylar rose and turned it off then pressed the speed dial on the phone.

"I'll call if I need you," Bob's voice said. "There's possibly two more to go off tonight." The foaling alarms attached to the mares went off once the animal had been down for twenty seconds, activating a receiver which then paged Skylar and Bob.

She excused herself to use the downstairs bathroom and on the way back, the spare key hanging on a hook by the back door snagged her attention. Would that placate the impatient man in her living room for the moment? It was a compromise. She took the key off the hook.

But the moment she walked back into the living room, the pager bleeped again. "That's number two," Bob said. "I'll call Zack up at the house."

"I'll call," she said quickly. The other boys had the night off so Zack, standing in for her, was on call. "You carry on, Bob. I'll alert the vet, too, in case we need him."

Zack was already pulling on his boots.

"I'll grab a jacket." She turned and started for the stairs but Zack grabbed her hand.

"No, you won't." He leaned forward and kissed her hard on the mouth. "Get some sleep. We'll continue this tomorrow."

It wasn't until after he'd closed the door that she realized she still had the key in her hand.

Skylar and Bob were in her office when Zack poked his head in the office door. "All set?" he asked Bob.

The two men were flying to Minneapolis to meet a friend of Bob's near Canterbury Park Racetrack. The man had a couple of well-bred broodmares for sale.

"Sure you won't come?" he asked as she walked them out to the truck they were taking to the airport.

Skylar shook her head. She wasn't keen on leaving the farm with Bob and Zack away. Anyway, she had paperwork to catch up on.

"Everything's done, the vet's happy with the foaling shed so you keep away," Zack ordered. "Dean's around. You've got my number, right?"

Sheesh! "Yes, Grandma," she drawled.

He opened the passenger door while Bob slid behind the wheel. "You cooking up anything tonight?" he asked in a sultry undertone.

"Hot dish, maybe." She grinned. The famous South Dakotan term *hot dish* referred to anything gooey cooked in one dish with cheese on top, but they both knew that wasn't what she meant.

"Ooh, baby," he whispered, and before she could slap him away, he leaned down and planted a firm kiss right on her lips. She took a quick step back and gave a furtive look around, feeling the heat burning her cheeks. With a wicked grin he climbed into the truck.

Tidying up the office might hopefully be an antidote to rampant sex hormones. Now was as good a time as any with Zack Manning glaring at her every time she got within a mile of anything with four legs.

She tore the tatty desk pad off to throw it in the trash but noticed the name *Burke* and a phone number, circled in Zack's handwriting.

She knew it was Zack's handwriting because of the note he'd taped to her front door when he'd finished foaling in the small hours. Her face lapsed into another dreamy smile. Not wanting to wake her, he'd said he and Bob would be starting late but she was not to help with the mucking out, the boys could handle it.

Talk about overprotective.

She leased some land from John Burke for her summer mares. The use of one hundred and fifty acres of pasture from the ex-hog farmer next door was good income. One day she hoped to be able to extend the twenty-eight stall broodmare facility so she could winter over more mares.

What could he want? She dialed but there was no reply.

The spring-cleaning took longer than expected but since Zack was going to be late anyway, Skylar was in no hurry. It was dark when she locked her office. She passed Dean and asked him to check that the foaling alarms were switched on; there were still a couple of mares close to their time.

It was usual for her to stop at Roscoe's paddock on the way home, but as she drew near, her ears picked up something weird. Nash had installed two or three lights along the driveway and they glinted dully off the stainless steel of the automatic livestock waterer.

She concentrated and then picked out a large dark shape on the ground, a couple of yards in from the fence.

Roscoe was down. Her first thought was colic. She'd seen it a hundred times. If it was just a bellyache, caused by change of feed or not drinking enough, a colicky horse sometimes lay down or stood stretched out, turning its head to nip and nuzzle its flanks.

"What's up, old boy?" she called to warn him she was coming. Roscoe lifted his head to peer at her, then dropped it again. His breathing wasn't particularly labored and she couldn't see if he was sweating. Probably just a mild case.

She climbed the fence, thinking to coax him up and

give him a bit of a walk around. It wasn't until she was squatting down beside him and put her hand on his stomach that the first real concern stirred in her gut. He was soaked in sweat. His upper lip curled right back and his eye gleamed white in the darkness.

She started to rise, hoping to catch Dean before he went up to the big house where Peggy always set dinner aside for him in the kitchen. It never occurred to her that the trusty old gelding she'd owned since she was three would hurt her. As the horse blew and then heaved himself toward her in a desperate effort to roll over, a front hoof caught her at the base of her neck and knocked her flying. Just as well, she thought in a crazy burst of lucidity, or he'd have rolled on top of her. That was her last thought before the back of her head caught the edge of the waterer.

Zack stopped the truck, his forehead creasing at the lack of lights on at the cottage. Dinner was definitely mentioned and Skylar was not so sensitive she would cancel just because he'd teased her.

He tapped the steering wheel, peering through the windshield at the dark windows. They'd arrived back a little earlier than expected and Zack was looking forward to seeing her. He'd already driven by the stables when he'd dropped Bob off. Her office was locked up and in darkness.

So he turned the truck in the direction of the big house. Maybe some news had come through about Patricia. It wasn't like Skylar to let people down. She had his number.

Case Fortune opened the door as he was about to ring the bell. Skylar's oldest half brother looked stern.

"Zack. I just knocked on your door."

"What's up?"

"My father and I were just discussing the gossip pages of the *Tribune* today."

His gut tightened. As far as he knew, the story his father had instigated hadn't broken yet.

"My sister's condition is attracting attention," Case continued. "It would be nice to think some progress was being made on an engagement announcement, some-time before the baby comes."

Zack swallowed with relief. "I'm working on it." His foot nosed the step as he tried to curb his impatience.

"Dad has got enough on his mind at the moment," Case continued. "The last thing he needs is the spot-light on the family. You are going to do right by Skylar, aren't you, Zack?"

"Is that because you give a damn or you're just wor-ried about the gossip rags?" He squared up to the bigger man.

Case raised his hands in peace. "Keep your shirt on. Of course I give a damn, she's my sister. But as CEO of Dakota Fortune, I also have an obligation to see that the reputation of the firm and my family members doesn't suffer."

"The way I see it, the Fortune name is dragged through the mud about once a week." Zack's voice crackled with annoyance.

"You might think about that next time you frequent one of the top restaurants in town," Case rumbled.

"Point taken." Zack peered around the other man's bulk at the open door. "You'll be the first to know when it happens, Case. In the meantime, it'd just be good to see her. Is she inside?"

Case shook his head. "I haven't seen her. Maybe she's gone to see Maya in town."

Zack turned in the direction of the stables, scowling. "She invited me for dinner but she's not home."

"Not like Skylar to renege on an invitation."

Zack started down the stairs at a brisk trot. "I'll go have another look at the stables. If she's gone against her word, I'll throttle her."

Case followed him swiftly down the stairs, looking concerned. "I'll come with you. What do you mean, gone against her word?"

They sped down the driveway. "I asked her to keep away from the horses and to stop riding till the baby was born. Too many hidden dangers."

"Gina and I are trying for a baby. The sooner the better, as far as I'm concerned."

Zack grinned wryly. "Well, congratulations, Case. Welcome to all this worry."

"Old Roscoe is having a roll in his paddock," Case commented as they slowed on the approach to the stable complex.

Dean and Bob were talking outside the mare barn. The stable hand told them he'd last seen Skylar five-to-ten minutes ago, on her way home. Bob made the comment she usually stopped by to see Roscoe in the evening.

Zack's heart dropped to his knees. He took off running toward Roscoe's paddock. They found Skylar groggily trying to drag herself away from Roscoe's thrashing body. Praying there were no spinal injuries, Zack vaulted the fence, grabbed a handful of jacket and pulled her a few meters away. The rest passed in a blur. It seemed an age later before he was in the backseat of

Bob's car with her cradled in his arms. Case was driving, the others staying back to tend to Roscoe.

Skylar squirmed and arched her spine.

"Keep still." Zack wrapped her up in his arms, tense as rock. "Where does it hurt?"

"Head," she mumbled. "Neck. Roscoe?"

"He'll be fine. Bob's with him." He felt a stab of pure hatred for the horse. He half hoped Bob would put a bullet in him.

"Zack?" Skylar's voice suddenly rang out clearly. There was no mistaking the fear.

He hugged her tighter. "Shh, baby. I've got you."

She moved her head slowly as if her neck was a piece of wood. A single tear slid down her cheek. "My baby?" Her voice broke.

He squeezed his eyes shut for a second. It was easier thinking about her or the horse than what might be going on with the baby. Forcing himself to be gentle when really he wanted to explode, he stroked her hair.

But she was disoriented and confused and kept mumbling the horse's name and the word *baby,* over and over.

White-faced and more terrified than he had ever been in his life, he bent his head and rested his lips on her hair. "It'll be fine, Sky. I promise."

They made the hospital in double-quick time. Case had driven one-handed while calling their predicament in on his cell phone. The second the car came to a halt, he leapt out and met the small cluster of nurses and doctors and they loaded her onto a gurney. With Case up ahead, loudly issuing orders, Skylar and Zack were soon inside an Emergency Department treatment room.

They took all her vital signs and questioned and

prodded her endlessly. Skylar was silent, fearfully so. Zack was frightened, too, right down to his marrow. He could not stop looking at her white face but he wouldn't let her see his fear, looking away every time she met his eyes. He knew she would not be taking much in and that he had to listen to the doctors for both of them.

Skylar was unable to say for sure if she'd been knocked out but her slightly confused state convinced the doctors that she had a concussion. The top of her shoulder and side of her neck were red and swelling and there was an egg-sized lump on the back of her head.

Of more concern was a possible abruption. A sharp jolt such as falling onto her back violently could have ripped part or all of the placental sac away from the womb, meaning the fetus would not be getting the blood and nutrients it required. But apparently there was no bleeding and did not appear to be any leakage of amniotic fluid. The doctor ordered an ultrasound and she was hooked up to a fetal monitor. Both of them were comforted to hear the mushy quick tones of their baby's heartbeat.

"That's a good sign, surely?" Zack squeezed Skylar's hand while tears of relief poured silently down her face.

More time passed. He told Case he may as well go home as there would be no news for hours.

"I'm probably far enough along that the ultrasound will show us what sex it is," Skylar suddenly said, her voice subdued.

Zack nodded. "Are you ready for that?" Personally, he couldn't bear knowing if the worst happened.

She considered the question, and incredibly, her mouth softened in a small smile. "Amanda, if it's a girl." She sniffed. "Don't know why."

Zack felt her nails digging into his palm and so many conflicting emotions tore about inside. His daughter. Amanda. Would she be tall, like her parents? Fair? He squeezed his eyes shut, trying to shut off the images of a small girl with Skylar's blue eyes and wide mouth. *Don't lose it now.* He had to stay focused and calm.

"Is that all right?" Skylar asked, and he heard the hope in her voice. He knew she was trying to distract them both.

"Amanda it is." He squeezed her hand.

"How many should we have?"

He stifled a groan. He would be happy with just this one, should the powers that be grant them a healthy baby. But he played along, wanting to comfort her. "At least a rugby team."

What started out as a watery smile soon dissolved into heartbroken tears and she squeezed her eyes shut.

"Hey, hey. Keep positive, love." He kissed her hair while she did a reasonable impression of being in labor, judging by the savage pressure she put on his hand. "You're in good hands here. I promise you it will be okay."

But really he knew that this was out of his control. He had never felt so helpless in his life. And although everything in him wanted to rage at the world, her misery and dependence on him kept him from doing so.

She let go of his hands and covered her face. "I can't bear it, Zack. I let you down. I couldn't keep your baby safe."

She apologized time and again for going into the paddock. "He was quiet, I thought he just had a bellyache. He didn't try to roll until I was beside him." A fresh bout of tears erupted. "I would never have…"

He took her hands in both of his and brought them

to his lips. "I know you wouldn't have." Yes, he was angry about that, too, but she didn't need guilt compounding her fears. "Sky, I can be strong for you, but you've got to be strong for the baby." He shook her hands lightly. "You hear me? There's no one to blame. It's just life." He stared hard at her, willing her to take heart.

Finally the ultrasound equipment arrived and the preparations were tense and silent. But then Zack saw the most beautiful thing he'd ever seen. Life, with its thumb in its mouth and unlikely looking extremities and features. The ultrasound technician considerately asked if they wanted to know the sex.

Zack felt Skylar's involuntary jerk, took in her wan, wanting face. Recognized that she needed this, needed the distraction of planning and hope. He nodded and it was hard to do, because he *so* did not want to know, did not want to bond any further with the baby should the worst happen.

They turned to the technician and the tears flowed down her face when they were told to expect a girl.

All the energy drained out of her then and she slept. By six in the morning, Zack's eyes burned with fatigue. He disengaged her hand, walked to the window and stretched.

Would she get over it if the baby died? He hated not being able to comfort her. It reminded him of his mother at the end when the drugs could not subdue the pain ripping her to shreds and she couldn't understand why they weren't working anymore.

Skylar's guilt was eating her alive. If the baby didn't make it, would she push him away so he didn't remind her of it? Should the unbearable happen, would she let him nurture her, take care of her? Give her more babies?

Zack realized with a jolt that his future happiness depended on her being there, baby or not.

Whoa! The lightening sky outside seemed to float through the window and fill his mind with cotton wool. Everything paled into insignificance. The scandal that was about to erupt back home, his fear that her family would keep her from marrying him, even the life of his baby.

All he wanted was for Skylar to emerge from this whole and strong and stand by his side.

"Zack?"

He spun around at the sound of her sleepy voice. When she held out her hand and smiled that sweet smile, Zack Manning came as close to weeping as he'd ever come in his life. She took his hand, moved the sheet aside and placed it on her abdomen.

"Now can you feel her?"

He felt her. Baby Amanda moved under fingers that had never felt so sensitized. Her tiny insistent prods completely overwhelmed him. They reached for each other at the same time and he wrapped her up tightly and lay his cheek against her wet face.

At eight o'clock, they were told they could go home, provided she rest up for the next few days. The doctor looked sternly at Zack's relieved face. "She must have someone with her constantly. You need to be aware of the danger signs."

"Danger signs?"

"Bleeding. Leaking of amniotic fluid, the vaginal plug, fever, pain.

Zack nodded and gave Skylar a grim look. "I won't let her out of my sight, believe me," he said with feeling.

"The main danger is infection. The jolt Ms. Fortune suffered may have thrown up a blood clot which the placenta is hiding. And then there is the concussion. She may feel nauseous, dizzy, have a bit of double vision. Anything more serious or more prolonged than that, we want her back here pronto." The doctor smiled at the relief on their faces. "But all the signs are good."

Eight

Skylar threw the sheets back and sat on the edge of the bed. Today, she would not take no for an answer. She was getting up and the heck with it.

Zack's fussing had driven her to distraction, especially when she'd overheard him yesterday telling Maya on the phone that she wasn't up to visitors. He had not left the cottage, barely left her room, for three days. She wanted to see Roscoe, who apparently had made a full recovery, and make sure Bob and the team were coping with the extra workload, since Zack was now spending all his time watching her like a hawk.

She showered and dressed, surprised he hadn't come in to check on her yet, shove that damn thermometer in her mouth or take her blood pressure with the gadget he'd had delivered. How long would he keep this up? she wondered, buttoning her fire-engine red jacket.

Totally overprotective. Heaven help the unlucky lad who came to pick their daughter up for her first date.

That thought made her smile as she descended the stairs, but she checked at the sound of his voice.

"I'm sorry, Dad, I can't get away. It's unavoidable."

Zack's back was to her. She considered briefly escaping out the door before he noticed, but something in his tone made her pause.

"No, I don't blame you. Just do your best to keep a lid on it. I need a few more days."

Skylar burned with curiosity. She'd gotten the distinct impression he and his father were not close.

Zack sighed heavily and began to turn toward where she waited at the bottom of the stairs. "If this gets out right now, it will have major implications for me." He saw her standing there and his whole demeanor changed. "Right, gotta go. Good luck." He broke the connection and stared at her. "Where do you think you're going?"

"Out," she said promptly. "To get some fresh air."

He moved forward and put a hand on her forehead. "You're a bit flushed."

"It's the jacket," she replied tartly, "reflecting my perfectly pregnant glow."

As expected, he refused to let her out the door until she had eaten and had her temperature, blood pressure and pupils thoroughly checked. "No pain? Nausea…" He ran through the long list of symptoms the doctor had warned him to be on the lookout for. "Just a half hour then," he said, finally satisfied. "And I'm coming, too."

They set off for a leisurely stroll through the trees toward the stables. It was all Skylar could do not to skip in the early summer sun. She felt she'd been let out of prison and could finally breathe. Although Zack hadn't said or done anything to show he blamed her for the accident, her own guilt had her walking on egg-shells around him. Her stupidity had given them both quite a scare.

"What's the problem with your father?"

Zack did not look at her.

"The phone call," she reminded him.

"No problem," he said shortly, frowning into the distance.

"What implications for you were you referring to?"

"Nothing I can't handle."

"Zack—" she expelled an impatient breath "—you say you want us to spend time together, get to know each other, yet every time I mention your family, you clam up. What are they, a bunch of axe murderers?"

Her attempt at humor elicited a cool gaze. "Very funny."

Skylar sniffed, her good mood evaporating in the sunlight. Okay, she may not be the most sophisticated conversationalist in the world, but she had a right to know more about him and his family. After all, his family was going to be her baby's family…

She opened her mouth to tell him so when his head snapped up and he pointed through the trees. "Someone's looking for you."

Roscoe nickered as they broke the line of trees and stepped out onto the driveway. After a few minutes being fussed over and petted, he trotted along the fence beside them as they walked. The vet had come straight out the night of the accident and administered mineral oil to clear the blockage in his intestines. He looked to be in no discomfort now.

All the boys crowded into her office, grinning and talking over each other to bring her up to date. Foaling was finished and it was just as well, Bob told her, as she'd need to get the alarms checked. He had tested the alarm before going to bed the night before but it hadn't activated. The last foal of the season had arrived unannounced during the night and, thankfully, none the worse for it.

One by one, they left to carry on with their chores. "Zack, if I promise not to leave the office, can I stay for an hour? Check the e-mails and pay some bills?"

Unexpectedly, he grinned down at her. "Writing checks is supposed to put your blood pressure up, isn't it?"

There were times when being around Zack Manning caused her blood pressure to go right through the roof and this was one of them. Her frustration about his overprotectiveness and reticence to discuss his family melted away. Awareness tickled along her spine, reminding her of his appeal. Lean-hipped, tightly defined muscles, long, strong legs. She grinned back, thinking if he was a stallion, she'd never get out of the receiving barn!

"What?" he asked when she snorted.

She waved him away, muttering that her blood pressure was just dandy, thanks. The moment the door closed behind him, she picked up her diary, flapping it in front of her burning face. Holy Toledo! When he smiled at her like that, with genuine affection and humor sparkling in his eyes, she wondered how she could deny him anything.

Her smile faded as silence descended. She wanted more than affection, much more. Because she was seriously considering his proposal.

Zack was the only man she had ever wanted, or slept with. He respected her as a breeder and was the one person apart from Patricia she felt she could rely on. They had much in common with their love of horses and the outdoors. Skylar thought his home was beautiful and a part of her had always regretted not traveling, seeing the world before setting herself up in a business that occupied all her time.

So what was she waiting for?

How could she? It was a ridiculous notion to run off with a virtual stranger, putting not only herself but her baby completely in his hands.

It was the attention, she supposed, scrolling disinterestedly through the mail. She enjoyed being the center of his attention. She had never felt that before. Robust good health and her disinterest in men meant her family barely noticed her existence.

Except Patricia. She missed her so much. Her father was right, Patricia would love to see her expecting, happy, in love. She was the one constant in Skylar's life, especially during the adolescent years when she felt the lack of a mother most keenly. Patricia had always built her up, noticed her, heaped praise on her head when no one else even knew if she was in the room.

Patricia would like Zack, and for no other reason than because Skylar did.

Pregnant women were supposed to want their mothers, she reflected. Yet she did not have the same burning desire to show Zack off, or show herself off, to Trina.

The phone rang, startling her. Talk about ESP! "I was just thinking about you," she told her mother.

"Blake told me what happened." Her mother had many voices and today's crackled with dry sarcasm. "I suppose it would have been too much to ask for a phone call from my baby doll's hospital bed."

"Sorry, Mother. I didn't want to worry you unnecessarily." She was surprised her mother could find time in her busy schedule to call.

"Sweetie, if you insist on making a grandmother of me, you could at least keep me up to date. Is everything all right?"

"Yes, I'm fine. A knock to the head, that's all."

"Well, darling, I have the perfect cure. I'm going on a cruise this weekend. Five days around the Caribbean. Why don't you join me? Good food. Sun and shopping and all the pampering you need at this time of your pregnancy. And," Trina's voice lowered conspiratorially "I'm sure we could find someone to make your Kiwi jealous enough to pop the question."

"Mother…" Skylar chided. You could count on Trina to manipulate a situation to her advantage. "Sorry. It's really not my scene."

There was silence. Quite a long and awkward silence. Skylar sat up a little straighter, slightly perturbed. Trina didn't do silence. "Mother?"

"Skylar, I know I haven't been much of a mother…"

Trina didn't do sentiment, either. "Is something wrong?" Amazingly, she felt concern, when exasperation was a more normal emotion toward her mother.

"Nothing. I'm being silly. Is everything really all right? How are your smelly horses?"

"Fine." If you didn't count all the little things going wrong lately, she mused, but it was strange that her mother would express an interest in the stud farm.

"And your father?"

Skylar chewed on her bottom lip, not sure how much,

if anything, Trina knew about Patricia's disappearance. As far as she knew, it hadn't hit the papers yet, but Skylar didn't bother much with the papers. "He's well. What is it, Mother? Why the sudden interest?"

"Can't a mother express an interest in her only daughter's life? Especially when she's expecting her first child?"

Skylar's distance from her mother originated from years of being let down. Birthdays forgotten, graduations not attended, weekend visits canceled because Trina had gotten a better offer...but despite all that, Skylar warmed at her mother's words. Maybe mothers and daughters did grow closer with the advent of children.

Surprising herself, she invited her mother to meet her for lunch in town before her vacation. It seemed Trina had something on her mind. The least Skylar could do was give her an hour of her time.

"Zack?"

Skylar's voice from the passenger seat jolted him back to reality, just as the car behind gave a sharp toot and he realized the lights had changed.

"I know what you were doing."

He accelerated smoothly, a small smile threatening to break loose. "Tell me you weren't," he challenged.

They were in town for Skylar's checkup and another ultrasound. Happily there were no bad effects from the accident and she had been given the green light to go back to work. Of course, his and her ideas about what constituted work were as wide as the Atlantic Ocean.

Sitting at the lights in Sioux Falls on the way home, a class full of kids—little ones, all with hands linked—had crossed the road in front of their car. They wore a maroon uniform with hats and shorts and cute little shoes. Some skipped in a clumsy sort of congo line. Some sang. One little girl with blond pigtails looked right in the window at him.

"I hope our girl looks just like her," he murmured. "A mini version of you."

"She's got no front teeth," Skylar protested.

Getting the all clear from the doctors was a relief. Watching the scan for the second time was just as magical. That was his baby, his flesh and blood in her belly, moving, sucking her thumb, yawning. It was over too soon. He wondered if he should invest in a home scanning machine so he could see it every day. He seemed to recall some big movie star or other had one.

Beside him, Skylar gave a little jerk and he glanced at her. "What is it?"

"Nothing," she reassured him. "She's squirming. At least, she's making me squirm."

"Man, that must feel…"

"It feels like—bubbles," she said happily, moving her hand over her belly.

"Like you've got wind?"

"No. Like exhilaration. When you've just had the best exciting news and you can't wait to tell someone because you know they're gonna be wowed." She gave him a sunny smile.

Something tugged at him, deep inside. Whatever the future held, he would not trade sharing this pregnancy with her for anything.

Later, she succumbed to an afternoon nap while Zack prepared dinner. Nagging her about marrying him wasn't an option while she recuperated, but the pressure was mounting. His father's phone call the day before re-

minded him that things he had no control over were
threatening to blow the lid on the pleasant domestic situation he was currently engaged in.

His father, John Carter, was living rough in the South
Island of New Zealand when Zack's private investigator had finally tracked him down. Bitter about the hand
life had dealt him, he initially wanted nothing to do with
his son. But when Zack heard his story, he persuaded
him he had the means to help in his quest for repara-
tion or revenge.

Together, father and son tracked down witnesses and
hired lawyers to bring a civil case against the Thorne
family, Zack's mother's family. But they hadn't bar-
gained on the Thorne's political clout. One-by-one, the
lawyers opted out, intimidated. The case floundered in
February, when Zack was in South Dakota the first
time, considering making a move on Skylar Fortune.

Zack spent a great deal of time and money hunting
down offshore lawyers from firms he hoped would not
be so easily put off. But a few weeks ago, frustrated by
the lack of progress, John Carter took matters into his
own hands. While Zack was in South Dakota, discovering Skylar's pregnancy, his father put into motion
plans that could irreparably harm the likelihood of them
sharing in the life of Skylar's baby. He'd contacted a reporter on a top current affairs TV show.

When Zack found out, he and his father persuaded
the reporter not to air the show right away. He doubted
he would ever get Skylar's, or her family's, agreement
to marry him with the scandal that his father was intent
on exposing.

Unfortunately, the government of New Zealand had
called a snap election and the reporter was putting the

acid on his father to air the show now. The scandal involved the leader of the opposition and there was a good chance the man could be the next prime minister of the country.

And that's why Zack had about a week to get his ring on Skylar's finger. Because when the news broke in Australia and New Zealand, the fallout would be huge. The Australian Fortunes would hear of it and as much as Max's father, Teddy, thought of Zack, he would feel it his duty to inform his American cousins of Zack's background.

Skylar came into the kitchen, her hair brushed out and still damp from her shower. She came up behind him and slipped her arms around his waist. Zack craned his neck around to peer at her. "Hungry?"

"Hungry for something," she murmured, pressing her face into his back.

He turned to face her, resting his hands on her shoulders. "You smell like apples." He bent his head to her hair, breathing in deeply. He'd noticed the apple-scented shampoos and lotions in her bathroom.

Skylar reached up and touched her lips to his tentatively. She pulled back, watching him. The kiss may have been uncertain but there was a candid and determined look in her eye.

Zack's mouth quirked. "You *are* hungry."

Her gaze dropped and she blushed. "I phoned the doctor when we got home. Asked him if it was safe to, you know…"

He waited, trying not to smile at her discomfort.

Skylar studied the buttons on his shirt. "If we could…"

"You rang the doctor to ask if we could have sex?"

She went even pinker. "'Resume sexual relations' was the phrase, I think."

"Why didn't you ask while we were there?"

Her shoulders raised in an embarrassed shrug.

Although they shared her bed, Zack heeded the hospital's warning that she take things easy for a few days. Just as well he was familiar with sheep, New Zealand's most populous livestock by far. Veritable flocks of them marched through his brain as he lay beside her, listening to her breathe, feeling her warmth, clasping his hands together to stop from touching her.

He nuzzled the base of her ear. "And what did the doctor say?"

"No swinging from the chandelier." She rubbed her cheek against his lips.

"Lucky." He nipped at her earlobe. "We don't have a chandelier." His fingers pressed in firmly up the length of her spine, a particularly sensitive spot, he'd discovered.

Sure enough, she arched into him. "You want to turn whatever's burning off?" Her fingers began undoing his shirt buttons. "I'm in rather a hurry."

Zack reached behind him and complied. Who was he to argue? "Hurry, huh? It's not good to keep a pregnant lady waiting."

"It's not," she affirmed, slipping her hands inside his open shirt and skimming his chest. "They get cranky."

Zack returned the compliment by making short work of the buttons on the front of her blouse, delighted to find she was not wearing a bra. She wore a sarong-type wraparound skirt that reached almost to her ankles. "You must be wearing a thong," he murmured, running his hands over her backside. "Can't for the life of me feel any panties under this very thin material."

Skylar rubbed against his groin, torturing him. "No panties."

He took her mouth and swallowed her gasps, his blood racing now. What had happened to his shy little virgin? Her tongue lashed his and he groaned into her mouth. "We're not going to make the bedroom if you keep this up."

"Good." She pulled back, her hands clutching both sides of his open shirt. She tugged him over to the dining table and used her toe to hook one of the chairs out to face them. Zack just had time to let the blind down and wonder if the door was locked before his impatient lover pushed him down into the chair.

"I can't wait." She leaned down and nipped at his mouth while deftly undoing the fastening of his jeans. "My hormones have gone sex mad."

Her breasts were right in front of his face, heavy, fragrant. Inviting. He leaned forward and took one large dark nipple into his mouth. She stopped what she was doing and arched closer.

"Oh, harder," she breathed, and tangled her fingers in his hair. "I can't bear it if you don't."

Zack obliged happily and transported her to a level of excitement he hadn't seen in her before. Busy as he was, he managed to push his pants down around his knees and started on the tie to her skirt, but she had other ideas. She stood over him and lifted the folds of material up until it bunched around her waist.

His body strained with excitement. She hadn't lied. No panties and no thong, either. He gripped her hips and she spread her legs and moved over him. Zack thought he'd died and gone to heaven when she dipped her knees and teased him over and over. He could barely contain his need to plunge deep, but this was about her. This was about her asking him, trusting him, blossoming in her newfound sensuality.

In the end, her greed won out and she resisted his firm grip on her hips and jerked down. They stilled, staring at each other and she looked unsure again, as if now that she had what she wanted, she didn't know what to do with it. Zack took the lead and lifted her arms above her head so she was stretched out above him.

Her breasts trembled in front of his mouth and she jerked again when he feasted on them. He felt her thighs bunch as she braced herself and began to slide up and down on him, her tight tummy brushing his chest.

It was hot and fast. Within seconds, her fingers gripped his hard and her breath came in rhythmic agonized moans. He suckled harder and fought to keep his control when she clenched hard around him, flooding him with her heat. Her lower body and legs stiffened, but her fingers slid limply from his and she slumped, gulping air, her damp face pressed against his neck.

Zack nudged her face around with his chin and took her unresisting lips in a long, carnal kiss. "I want you up again. Slower, this time." He burned with the need to climax but first he wanted to test the theory that pregnant women were prone to multiple orgasms, something to do with increased blood flow to the extremities.

After a long, slow loving, their mouths and eyes locked on each other the whole way, she succumbed to a shivering climax that seemed to go on and on. Only then did he firm his hands on her hips and thrust strongly up while she clung to his neck and rode him. Zack climaxed hard, digging his heels into the floor, every muscle rigid, yet boneless inside where the ecstasy swirled and licked and nibbled into every cell.

Bathed in sweat, he wrapped her up in his arms, swaying and rocking. Thank God for sturdy chairs.

After dinner, they lay in bed chatting idly. Zack raised up on his side and placed his hand on Skylar's sweetly rounded white belly. Their daughter obediently kicked on command. They lay for a long time, watching for the telltale little movements on her skin. A little bump appeared, then nothing for a minute, then again in a different place. Skylar directed his hand to different parts of her belly and he was enthralled by the activity under his fingers. "This isn't because we made love, is it?"

She smiled. "She's just letting us know she's there and she's great." She blinked at a particularly strong kick. "I'm going to be black-and-blue inside."

"It must feel amazing. For the first time, I feel like women are the lucky ones."

"You won't be saying that at the birth," she told him with a grimace.

Zack questioned her endlessly on how her body was changing, her moods, her tastes. Cheated out of the first few months of this pregnancy, he wanted to know every detail.

"I hope I'll be a good mother." Skylar sighed, nestling into his side. "I was just thinking yesterday how sad it would be if little Amanda thought about me the way I feel about my mother."

"No chance," Zack told her and then felt ungracious. He hardly knew the woman. But his own mother sacrificed everything for him and it was hard not to feel strongly about the type of woman who would leave her child feeling unwanted. It may not have been Trina's idea to leave her children with Nash, but she could have fought for them and involved herself a lot more in her daughter's life.

"Thing about mothers," Skylar continued lazily, "they're the people in the world most everyone has regrets about. My mother is selfish and shallow, but sometimes I think she has her regrets, just like everyone else."

"At least it's shown you how you don't want to be." Zack gave private thanks that Skylar recognized her mother's shortcomings and seemed determined not to repeat them. Her core values were much too wholesome to be impressed by beauty and wealth.

"What was your mother like?"

"Bossy." He was so relaxed and content, it didn't even occur to him to deflect her. He stroked her tight bulge, spreading his hand wide. "Strong."

Zack had loved and admired his mother, but there had been only the two of them. Close relationships were hard to forge when you moved every year. Gill Manning had been demanding and she had expected high standards of him but he had never once felt unloved or unwanted.

The only time she ever let him down was the day she sided with Rhianne's parents. Even so, he understood where she was coming from. She'd worked hard to provide for him. Watching him throw away the chance to go to university and make something of himself was intolerable for her.

Pressing his fingers down into Skylar's tummy gently, he sucked in a breath. "Feel that? She's really going for it."

A lump formed in his throat as he felt the tiny prodding against his fingers. "God, she's so... Can I listen?"

He shifted down and laid his ear on her stomach. There was that squishy heartbeat again and tiny, otherwordly thumps as his baby kicked. He was glad Skylar could not see his face. She couldn't begin to comprehend the emotion swamping him at this moment. His baby, inside her womb. His baby, feeding, beating a tattoo on her mother's insides. His baby breathing and sucking her thumb. Yawning and stretching. He closed his eyes tightly and the sounds intensified as his senses adapted to blindness.

Everything he had achieved, everything that made him the man he was came down to this, the tiny life inside the body of this surprising and warm woman he was sated with loving. The years of bitterness about what he had lost faded into nothing as Zack basked in contentment. He would give his life, gladly, for the tiny soul pressed against his ear and for the woman nurturing her. More than anything he wanted to keep them both safe.

"Can you hear her?" Skylar whispered.

Zack opened his eyes and nodded. He wouldn't give them up, he thought with a ruthless determination usually reserved for the boardroom. Either of them. He pressed his nose into her fragrant skin, surprised that she was fast becoming as vital to him as the baby she carried. He had not expected that.

Her hands moved on his head. "Zack? Why haven't you had babies before?"

He swallowed, toying with the idea of telling her about Rhianne. Toying with the idea of telling her everything. They were closer now and time was running out for him.

How much faith did he have that she would stand by him? Quite a bit, he conceded, but he didn't trust her family. He needed her agreement to marry him before his father's story hit the airwaves and her family stepped in and cut him out.

But if he told her about Rhianne, she might understand how much this baby meant to him.

And how much she meant to him.

There were similarities to his feelings for Rhianne and Skylar. Somehow they both pulled at him. Two girls from wealthy domineering families who'd had their lives mapped out and did not know where they stood in the world. Somehow that touched him, more than all the girls and women in between. Executives, stewardesses, professional women, fun-loving women… No one else had ever dragged out the tenderness and protectiveness from the brash boy who started off on the wrong side of the tracks and now ran his own empire.

Zack took a deep breath. "I got a girl pregnant once," he began.

Her hands, stroking idly through his hair, stilled.

Nine

This wasn't his first baby.

She lay perfectly still, frozen by a familiar disappointment, that of never quite making the grade. She wanted to be his first.

First baby, first love.

Zack moved back up the bed and onto his side, raised up on his elbow. "She was sixteen, still in school. I was a couple of years older and about to go to university."

The fist clutching her heart eased a little. It was a very long time ago.

"But I didn't fit the image of the man that her parents wanted for their precious, wealthy daughter."

Bitterness hardened his voice. Skylar turned onto her side also so she could watch his face.

"They offered us money to leave town. When my mother refused, they threatened to have my scholarship annulled and see to it that every university in the state would bar me." He cleared his throat. "They had the power to do that. We, my mother and I, had no power. It was as simple as that."

"What was her name?"

"Rhianne. Rhianne Miller."

"What happened?"

"They persuaded her to have an abortion."

"Oh, Zack." No wonder he was so overprotective, so determined not to let her out of his sight. Her eyes brimmed. To think she had withheld her pregnancy from him for so long. How could she make it up to him?

His eyes met hers briefly then he looked around the room, settling on each corner, as if he didn't want her to see his pain. "I didn't blame her for not sticking by me. I wasn't much of a catch back then. But all these years, I've wondered about my son or daughter, what he or she would have been like. How different my life might have been had he or she lived." The muscles worked in his jaw. "That was hard to swallow."

Skylar felt a little chill and her hands went involuntarily to her tummy. She knew, especially after her accident, she'd never get over losing a baby.

"It taught me one thing. I never wanted to be poor and at someone else's mercy again."

How appalled he must have been when history repeated and he found himself in the same situation. "Did you never meet anyone else you wanted to have a baby with?" Surely he must have had other lovers in the ensuing years, other relationships. She might wish she was the only one but that was unrealistic. The guy was in his midthirties.

He shook his head. "I nearly got engaged once but I

realized at the last minute I didn't feel enough for her. It wasn't like it was with Rhianne. It never was."

Do you feel it with me? How she wanted to ask but this was his story. His heartbreak. She wouldn't make it about her. "I'm so sorry I didn't tell you earlier, Zack. About the baby."

His face tensed up again. He leaned over her and reached out to cup her face with firm hands. "I won't lose this baby, Skylar," he grated. "I know what it's like to grow up in a one-parent family, to have the wealthy, the old money, look down their noses. I won't have—" his eyes slid down to her midriff "—Amanda suffer that, as well."

She didn't blame him but felt it was unfair to compare her family with Rhianne's. Anyway, Skylar had no intention of allowing her family or anyone else to dictate to her. "I'm not like that. Nobody here looks down on you."

"Prove it." He eyes glinted like steel. "Say you'll marry me."

She gazed at him for several moments, wavering, so close to saying yes. So close to trusting her inexperienced heart. But a slide in her belly cautioned her that it wasn't just her life she was impacting on. "I want to…" She squirmed out of his grasp and jammed herself into his side, so he couldn't see her face. Having heart-to-hearts, face-to-face made her cringe.

"I just—I'm not sure yet. But I promise, Zack, I am considering it very, very seriously."

He put his arms around her then, but the tension in the set of his jaw and the tightness of his chest as he appeared to sleep kept her awake for a long time. She closed her eyes and prayed for the courage to take that step.

Skylar felt she'd been largely ignored by her parents and siblings. She'd grown to be comfortable with it, but she could never accept that from Zack. He may be attentive and protective of her now but in two years or five or ten, would she be left sitting in his beautiful home alone while he was off having fun with his daughter and excluding her?

Or worse, off with another woman, one he could love like he loved Rhianne?

When she had given up everything she knew, would she still be left with nothing?

Late the next afternoon, Skylar was watching Zack's home movie when the phone rang.

"What are you up to?"

She sighed at the sound of Zack's voice.

"Same thing I was doing when you called the last time."

Three phone calls already and he had only been gone since lunchtime. He had driven over to Deadwood to meet with a breeder staying at Blake's casino.

"I'm on my way home now. Do you want to eat out?"

"I'll fix something. Maya's coming over for a visit after school." Maya taught at the grade school in the city. Skylar was looking forward to company.

She put the phone down and couldn't help smiling and patting her belly. "That's your daddy," she whispered. "Driving us nuts."

Even though it was exasperating, his constant checking up, insisting she rest and keeping her from her work, it still made her smile. She was the most pampered mother-to-be in the world. Zack would never let her down. She sensed he was the one person she could always rely on. A pretty great trait for a father, she thought. Her treacherous brain added *husband* to that.

She sat down and turned the DVD back on. This was the second time she had watched it today. Following his tour through the large modern house, she admired and considered the decor and layout of the rooms. Even imagined herself there moving about his kitchen, lying in his overmasculine bedroom or sitting on handsome wooden outdoor furniture by the pool.

She had it bad. Aside from his growing impatience with her dillydallying about marriage, they were closer in the days since the accident. He deserved an answer, some sort of definite commitment to their future.

His stud operation was impressive, much larger than hers, though he was still in the process of setting it up. She marveled at the state-of-the-art stables, more modern than anything she had seen.

That was another thing about Zack Manning Skylar admired. When he did something, he did it well. She'd had ample opportunity to see that in the way he tackled everything. From helping Bob run the stables in her stead, to cooking and looking after her—and don't get her started on the bedroom.

Skylar didn't know if she suffered from a surfeit of sex hormones or was just an overenthusiastic late starter. She was insatiable where sex with Zack was concerned. He was in danger of being attacked every time he walked into the cottage.

Not that she'd heard him complaining.

Maya, hidden behind a huge basket of goodies, interrupted the DVD. There was fruit and chocolate, baby clothes and creams and potions for stretch marks. "Have you been talking to Eliza?" Skylar asked. She had suffered several phone calls from her half sister about taking proper care of herself.

She poured glasses of iced tea and they opened some candy and watched the DVD. Maya was loud in her approval of Zack. It seemed every time Skylar turned around, someone was raving on about how great he was, how lucky *she* was.

Just once, it would be nice to hear it the other way around.

"It looks great," Maya enthused. "Can't wait to visit."

"Don't you start," she grumbled. "I wish everyone would stop pushing me to what they all see as a logical conclusion."

"You're crazy about him. It's obvious."

"Maybe so," she admitted. "But it'd be nice to know he was crazy about me, too."

"Would he ask you to marry him if he wasn't?"

Skylar cradled her tummy. "He's definitely in love with this little thing," she said softly. "You should have seen him last night, lying with his head on my tummy, listening to her move."

"Oh, wow!" Maya gave a loud sniff.

Skylar looked up in surprise. Her friend's beaming smile of a moment ago had vanished. She was on the verge of tears. "What is it?"

Maya wiped her eyes. "Mom would so love to see you like this. If only we could get word to her. She'd be home in a minute."

"I miss her heaps but it must be so much harder for you."

"I'm so scared," Maya whispered. "I just can't see why she'd go without a word. What can be so bad that she can't even tell me?"

Maya was Patricia's only child. It had always been just the two of them until they'd moved to the Fortune Estate. Patricia took on the job of looking after Nash's children after he kicked Trina out. Although the two younger girls quickly became friends, Maya wasn't so close to the other Fortune children. The boys and Eliza were old enough to remember Trina's manipulations and regarded Patricia and Maya with some suspicion.

"Dad will find her," Skylar reassured her. "All the boys have people working on it. In fact it's nice to see them and Blake all pulling together for Dad's sake. Whatever's gone on in the past, everyone wants Patricia home where she belongs."

Maya looked wistfully into her tea. "She was so happy when Nash retired and they took that trip to Australia. It was soon after they returned that everything changed. She seemed worried and distant. I wish I knew…"

"Skylar," a male voice called from the door.

"Oh, no," Maya groaned. "Creed."

Skylar made a face at her and went to open the door. "What brings you here?" Her siblings rarely visited her at the cottage.

"Oh, you know," Creed hedged, looking guilty. "Just passing."

She stared at him. "Zack sent you, didn't he?"

Creed couldn't hide his grin. "Be thankful he's so—attentive."

She stood back to let him in, shaking her head. "I don't believe him."

Creed stopped, his grin fading fast when he saw Maya on the sofa. "Maya." He gave her a brisk nod.

She reciprocated coolly. Skylar always felt uncomfortable around these two. They seemed to spark off each other and often ended up arguing. It had been that way as long as she could remember.

"Want some iced tea or something?" She fetched another glass when Creed nodded. "We were just talking about Patricia. You haven't heard anything from Dad, have you?"

Creed shook his head somberly. "Nothing as far as I know."

Maya heaved a big sigh.

"You have to give these things time, Maya," he said, accepting Skylar's drink with a roll of his eyes.

"She's my mother," Maya retorted. "I can understand her not contacting you but why take it out on me?"

Creed sighed and turned to Skylar. "You don't suppose Trina would have anything to do with this, do you?"

She looked baffled. "How?"

"I don't know. She does seem to have the knack of getting under everybody's skin."

Skylar was well aware of her mother's shortcomings. Trina delighted in causing mischief since being banished from the estate. It wasn't enough that her prenup was generous and Nash cared for the children she would have found to be a burden. She was bitter at losing her social status. Just in the last few months, she'd sold several untrue stories to the Sioux Falls social pages, even lying about Blake, her own son. Trina thought only of herself.

"Patricia knows what she's like, and she's too sensible and too secure to let Trina upset her."

Maya sniffed. "Sky's right. Mom is more likely to be upset by you or Case than Trina."

Creed jutted his chin out. "What is that supposed to mean?"

Maya got smartly to her feet and faced him. Skylar
blinked to see her friend's heated pout and clenched
fists. Surely they weren't going to resort to fisticuffs, as
they sometimes had as children.

"You know very well what I mean, Creed." Maya's
voice was carefully controlled and cold. "Ever since
Mom and I came to live here, you've never welcomed
either of us. You and Case thought my mother was just
another Trina."

Before Skylar could voice her protest, the two of
them let fly, just like old times. Creed shouted and Maya
dropped her aloof stance and shouted back.

Skylar sat back, openmouthed, amazed at how fast
the argument got out of hand. This was totally over the
top for the provocation. Maya's brown eyes flashed and
snapped with temper, and Creed inflamed the situation
by stepping forward with each forceful missive. They
were soon face-to-face and only inches apart, both breathing heavily.

Zack walked in, an incredulous look on his face.
"What the hell's going on?"

"Don't ask me," Skylar murmured, still overwhelmed by the passion of the argument.

Zack moved to her side quickly. "You all right?"

She nodded.

He turned back to glare at Creed. "I could hear you
two from Deadwood."

"Maya's a little upset," Creed said smoothly, overriding Maya's muttered apology.

"*I'm* upset?" she snapped back. "Damn right. I
wouldn't put it past you to have said something. I know
you don't think she's good enough for your father."

"I think nothing of the sort."

"Just because Sasha dumped you for Blake, you can't stand to see anyone happy."

They were off again, voices rising like applause at a baseball game. Creed flung a heated barb about Maya's on-again, off-again boyfriend and then Zack pushed between them. "Out! Both of you."

"Zack," Skylar protested, more interested in seeing where Creed and Maya were going with their passionate argument.

He ignored her. "Out, now. You're upsetting Skylar."

"For Pete's sake—" She began to protest but he cut her off.

"I mean it."

Everybody stared at him, and then Maya bent and picked up her bag. "It's time I was going anyway."

"Maya, don't go," Skylar entreated, scowling at Zack's face.

Her friend stalked to the door.

Creed threw his arms in the air, sighing heavily. "Maya, I'm—sorry."

Maya tossed a look over her shoulder. "You're sorry. You're always sorry, until the next time."

She looked at Skylar and Zack. "I'll call you, Sky. Take care."

Creed stepped forward, wincing as the door banged behind her.

"Where do you get off," Skylar rounded on Zack, "ordering people out of my house?"

"I won't have you upset—" he began, but she cut him off.

"The only person upsetting me right now is you." She turned to the door. "I'm going after her."

But on the way to the door she threw a scathing look

in Creed's direction and caught a glimpse of such desolation in her half brother's face, she quickly forgot about being mad at Zack. Desolation and something else, the same thing she had glimpsed at the restaurant but wasn't sure of then. Longing. He had spoken of unrequited love.

Creed was in love with Maya.

She was sure of it. Did Maya know?

"Creed?"

He blinked and it was gone.

Skylar opened the door, calling out as Maya got into her car. "Maya. Wait up." She caught up with her friend. "What's going on with you and Creed?"

"He just…he brings out the worst in me." She inhaled deeply, still visibly agitated. "I'm sorry if we upset you."

Skylar waved her apology away. "Maya, I think if you just opened your eyes, you'd see that Creed cares for you. He's got his own investigator trying to find Patricia, too."

Her friend snorted. "He's only looking for something incriminating. Nothing would please him more if he found something to discredit us."

They halted their conversation when their subject came out of the door. Creed gave them a long cool look on the way to his car.

"I think you're wrong," Skylar murmured as they watched his car move off. "He's not as bad as you think he is. As *I* thought he was."

"I wish I could believe that," Maya grumbled.

Zack's cell phone bleeped at four-thirty in the morning, waking both of them. At the sound of Max Fortune's somber voice, he was wide-awake in seconds.

"Wassup?" Skylar mumbled groggily as he eased out of bed.

"Business." Zack dragged on his jeans and headed for the door. "Go back to sleep."

Max was watching the evening news in Australia and thought Zack should know, regardless of the time. It was as bad as it could get. The current affairs TV show had scooped everyone, reneging on its promise not to air his father's interview until the eve of the New Zealand elections.

The country's foremost political family, including the current leader of the opposition, Zack's uncle, was drowning in allegations of blackmail and corruption. The government was overjoyed and Zack's name was back in the limelight, big-time.

"I thought your old man was dead," Max said.

"So did I." Zack switched on the television and turned the volume down with the remote.

"It sounds like a bad soap opera. Framed for a murder he didn't commit…"

Zack grunted and flicked through the international news channels. "Oh, he did it, but it was self-defense. The family bribed the three witnesses, had the police plant evidence and prejudiced the judiciary. It should have been manslaughter."

"How long for murder in New Zealand?"

His eyes flicked over a headline: *Historical conviction sinks New Zealand opposition party.* "Thirteen years, give or take." He chuckled mirthlessly. "He learned a few bad habits inside and continued on his winning ways."

"So that's why you moved to the South Island? To keep an eye on him?"

"I wanted to support him, help him."

By throwing money at him when all the old man really wanted was revenge. But all of Zack's money and desire to help could not prevent the demise of the court case.

"Does Skylar know any of this?"

"Dad had already done the interview by the time I found out I was going to be a daddy. The snap election was out of the blue. I thought I had a few more days up my sleeve."

Max exhaled. "Zack, do you want to marry her?"

"Yes!"

"Why?"

Zack considered for a moment. "It started off just being about the baby." And because he hoped a grandchild might make up for the crap hand his father had been served.

"Zack?"

He quickly changed channels and twisted around to frown at Skylar. "Did I wake you?"

She shook her head, yawning. "Anything wrong?"

"No, baby. Just some stock market stuff."

"Oh." She yawned again. "'Kay." She shuffled off toward the stairs like a sleepwalker.

"You know, Zack, when I recognized that Sky was falling for you, I almost warned her off. Not because I've ever seen you treat a woman badly, but you charm a woman into thinking it's her idea to keep things casual." Max chuckled. "I had you pegged as the world's biggest commitmentphobe."

"I'm committed," Zack muttered. He stared at the stairs where Skylar's sleepy form had ascended a few seconds before. His word should be enough for Max.

Although they rarely discussed personal feelings, Max knew him better than anyone.

"This isn't going to look good on your CV as far as the Fortunes are concerned," Max told him.

"Any chance you can keep Teddy from telling Nash? At least until I get a commitment from her. I think once we're engaged, the family might close ranks and support me."

"A fait accompli," Max mused. "I'll try but he and Nash have grown close. They're in almost daily contact since Patricia left. Dad thinks the world of you, but…"

"But blood is thicker than water," Zack finished for him. Especially, he thought, in a family like the Fortunes. Hadn't he experienced that sort of snobbery before? Another girl, another pregnancy, another wealthy family who liked to run roughshod over everyone.

Zack couldn't take the chance of the family turning their backs, not when his baby was at stake.

"Regardless of whether I can persuade my father to keep quiet," Max continued, "there is another problem. A couple of people rang the offices today, looking for you. The girls didn't know your whereabouts was a secret. Since every reporter in Australia and New Zealand wants to talk to you, it could be one or two of them are winging their way to South Dakota right now."

Ten

Zack's mood worsened the next morning when Skylar arrived at the stables, wittering on about Maya and Creed. She'd called Eliza last night and cooked up some harebrained scheme to throw the unassuming couple together alone, with no escape. Zack told her she ought to keep her nose out of it.

He was tired of waiting. The phone call from Max reminded him he'd given her all the leeway he could afford. As soon as he could get away, he strode to the office, just as she yanked open the door and started out.

Slapping the grain and dust from his thighs he looked at her face and stilled, seeing her distress. "What's up?"

It started to rain. Skylar had the car keys in her hand but backed up into the office, motioning him inside. "Someone's bought the pasture I lease from next door."

He followed her in. "What does your contract say?"

She looked down, scuffing her boot. "No contract. It was an informal arrangement."

Zack rubbed his hand over his stubbled face; he didn't bother shaving here until the day's work was done. "If you don't mind my saying, that's a funny way to do business."

"Yes, thank you, Zack," she muttered. "At the time, it suited us both. He was well paid."

She jingled the car keys in her hand.

"Where are you going?"

"I'm meeting a land agent in town. He's going to show me some plots."

"Now?" He was all fired up to talk about a different kind of deal.

"I need to find somewhere for the sixty mares I have booked this summer. This will lose me clients by the truckload."

Suddenly his brain cleared. "If you think about it, this couldn't have come at a better time. Maybe it's a good opportunity to scale the operation down."

Her head rose sharply. "Scale it…" She sounded disbelieving. "Whatever I decide to do, Fortune Stud will not be downgraded to some sort of hobby farm."

Zack wasn't in the mood to hear about Fortune Stud. He'd cooled his heels enough the last two weeks. "You have—" his eyes dropped pointedly to the tight roundness of her belly "—different responsibilities now. Be realistic, Skylar. It's time you were making arrangements. Call your clients and tell them to arrange alternative accommodations for their mares."

Skylar squared off and planted her boots, eyes sparking.

"Or, since you clearly don't like that idea, give Bob the responsibility. Make him manager. You have bigger things to think about."

"I don't have time for this." She huffed out an impatient breath and turned to the door.

Zack took a step and nailed her arm in a firm grip. *Oh, no, lady, you don't walk away from this.* "I want an answer, Sky," he told her grimly. "And I want it tonight."

Skyar raised her chin and met his uncompromising gaze. She knew exactly what he was talking about and it had nothing to do with Fortune Stud. How did they go from discussing her problems with the land to his marriage proposal? So much for a sympathetic ear!

The driving rain did nothing to improve her mood on the way into town. She felt disconnected lately, as if she'd been picked up and dumped into someone else's life and it wasn't just the pregnancy. She was not used to work-related calamities. Everything usually ran like clockwork around here but in the last few weeks, so many weird things had occurred. Nuisance things, nothing of any real importance but things that made her look unprofessional and could impact on business.

Was it hormones stoking her imagination, or was someone trying to sabotage her operation?

She considered the other thoroughbred breeders in South Dakota but there were so few of them. The Fortunes were prominent in business—maybe someone had a beef. But they would be more likely to target Case and Creed than her.

Who could profit from her loss of business? As she drove, her mind veered away from a nasty little suspicion that whispered and nagged. All through her consultation with the land agent she forbade herself to think of it, but it taunted and distracted her.

Zack Manning had something to gain if her business suffered.

If someone had designed this campaign of mischief to discourage her, it was working. She had built up a strong business since leaving college. She and her father invested heavily in expanding and refurbishing the facilities and when her gamble on Black Power paid off, she'd earned as credible a name in this industry as any young female had, even if her surname did open a few doors.

The land agent opened a big black umbrella and led her out to his car. Zack was right. She had other responsibilities now. But maybe he was banking on her seeing it would be simpler to make a fresh start if things were going wrong here. A fresh start in a new country.

"Are you all right?" the land agent asked. "You're a little pale. Morning sickness?"

Skylar shook her head. "Past all that."

Who had bought the land? Her neighbor, John Burke, said the buyer wished to remain anonymous and had gone through an agent. He apologized but said he'd left two messages. She hadn't gotten back to him.

Because of the accident and then being wrapped in cotton wool by the father of her baby…but there hadn't been any messages.

Suddenly she recalled Zack's handwriting on her desk pad. Burke's name and the phone number. The man *had* called, only no one—certainly not Zack—had told her.

She was getting this out of context. Everyone was entitled to the benefit of the doubt.

They drove to a second property but already Skylar knew it was unsuitable due to its distance from the estate. How could she look after sixty mares and foals if she lost the land? They got out of the car for a minute but the umbrella promptly turned inside out by a gust of wind.

"Tornado weather," the man said pleasantly. Many around here worried about tornadoes at this time of year after a cluster of devastating storms a couple of years back.

Was Zack Manning a tornado, ripping through her carefully structured life, sucking up her options so that starting anew with him seemed like the obvious answer?

An icy dread lodged under her ribs and she hugged herself.

The cardinal sin for shy people was to believe that one day their peers would seek them out and see how animated and interesting they really were. Skylar learned early not to draw attention to herself.

Zack's attention and concern for the baby had deluded her into thinking it extended to her, too. It was easy to visualize how good it could be between them, how right. She'd allowed herself to hope they had a future together.

The land agent chattered on but she kept mostly silent on the way back to his office, wondering how she'd suddenly found herself in love. Skylar Fortune who never looked at a man twice, who actively avoided situations where romance might flourish.

And the man she had finally accepted into her heart was trying to ruin her.

"The weather sure has set in. You drive careful now."

She nodded, opening the door against the deluge. That was another thing about love, she thought, turning away from the man with a listless wave.

The rain streamed down her face as she unlocked her car and slid inside.

Love hurt.

* * *

Darkness chased her home, even though it was only late afternoon. Her thoughts were dark, too, as was Zack's face when she opened the door and found him on the phone, pacing her living room. He stopped when she entered, his eyes unreadable from across the room, and then he turned away. She peeled her wet jacket off and heard him mutter something about having no comment to make.

Was he cooking up something here in her own house?

"What's wrong?" she asked when he snapped his phone shut and faced her.

"Nothing." He crossed the room and took her jacket, hanging it up on the hook. "You're wet."

"A little." He was tense, his face drawn and pale. Concern and worry rose up.

Dammit! That's what made this love thing so sickening and—girlie. Here she stood, worried to death about him while he was likely trying to ruin her.

Skylar averted her face, afraid he'd see the foul suspicions in her eyes. "Who was on the phone?"

"No one. Where have you been?"

She walked over to the gas fire, warming her hands. "Told you. With the land agent."

He grunted and leaned against the edge of the sofa, his arms folded across his chest.

"Your mother called."

"Oh, heck!" Skylar clapped a hand lightly against her forehead. The lunch date with her mother… "Was she mad?"

A brief rise of his shoulders.

"I'll have a snack," she decided, "and then go."

His brows beetled. "It's pouring out there and nearly dark. Just call her."

Skylar stared into the fire and considered that option hopefully. She wasn't thrilled about going back out into the rain but... "She's going on vacation tomorrow. I need to see her."

Straightening, she walked into the kitchen and opened the fridge, looking for something quick and easy. The back of her neck prickled when Zack stood behind her, close enough to feel the anger emanating out of him.

"We have things to discuss tonight...."

"Creed thinks she may have something to do with Patricia's disappearance. I want to see her face." She paused and tossed him a meaningful look over her shoulder. "I can generally tell when someone's lying."

Zack's gaze narrowed. "Skylar, this is just one more reason, one more excuse to keep me at arm's length. If it's not work, it's your family or your friend to fix up. It's one step forward and two back with you."

She shrugged. "I'm sorry. I have a lot on my mind right now."

"What's it going to take to get a simple answer from you?"

She banged the fridge door shut, annoyance tickling her throat. How come he got to make all the demands? "Maybe I want some answers, too. Why are you pushing so hard, Zack? Because I don't buy the illegitimacy thing."

He raised his head imperiously. "Shall I remind you of your father's wishes on that subject? Your brothers, also, haven't been slow to point out to me the importance of the family reputation."

She knew all that but she'd bet her lucky horseshoe that

the Fortune reputation was not the main thing concerning him. "Those are bows to your arrow, Zack, but they're not what's driving you to be so insistent on a quick wedding."

He paused, measuring her up. "I told you about Rhianne. I won't let you or your family cut me out of this baby's life. Not twice in one lifetime."

"You must know I would never keep her from you."

"Then commit. Announce it to the world."

Skylar shook her head in exasperation. "You want to pick me up and dump me in some godforsaken place I never even heard of before I met you, and you expect me to be chafing at the bit?"

This was getting them nowhere. She took a glass down from the shelf and filled it with water.

Zack leaned against the counter, his eyes on her face. "I'm not happy about it but I've already decided you can stay here until after the baby's born. I don't want you flying that distance at this stage of your pregnancy."

"You're taking a bit much on yourself, aren't you?" she began, fighting to rein in her temper.

"It means I'll have to go back and forth," he interrupted. "But if that's what it takes to get a commitment out of you…" He stopped and looked at her. "Will that make it easier?"

Skylar thought she might just explode. "*You've* decided?" she seethed. "*You* don't want me to fly?"

His chin lifted. "But if I'm going to be in and out of the country, I want a public announcement of our engagement. That way, I'll know you won't disappear on me."

Skylar banged her glass down on the counter, imagining it was his head. He wasn't taking a bit of notice. She might as well have been in the next room!

She forced herself to take a couple of deep breaths and count to ten. Nothing would be gained by losing her temper. "It's more than that, Zack," she said, striving for a more reasonable tone. "My business is very important to me."

"Skylar, you made it a success here, you can do it again somewhere else."

He wasn't taking the bait. Wasn't giving her anything tangible to grasp on to. If only he'd say that he loved her or even really liked her. "There is so much I don't know about you. I need to be sure what sort of family I'm buying into. Your family is going to be your daughter's family. You won't speak of your father…"

His head rolled back in a gesture of impatience. "You said you hoped you were a better mother than yours. I could say the same about my father. What our parents did, how they managed, or mismanaged, their parental responsibilities has nothing to do with us."

He came to her and grasped her shoulders. "Who have you been living with the last couple weeks? We're good together, Skylar. It's more than most people start with."

He had an answer for everything, except the things she really needed to hear. "This isn't bringing us any closer to an agreement, Zack," she told him sadly. "You're not giving me anything different. Anything that gives me hope for our future together."

"You're doing it again," he snapped. "Grasping at straws. Every time I try to get close to you, you fire a different shot. What's next, I wonder?"

"Did you buy that land?"

The second the words were out of her mouth, she regretted them. And in the long seconds when her quiet words hung in the air between them, she thought wildly that she didn't want to know. She did not want to hear he could be so underhanded. It was bad enough being a girl in love without knowing that she'd fallen for a sly manipulator.

Zack looked stunned. "What are you on about now?"

She nearly wavered. *Take it back,* whispered through her mind. But to not know was burying her head in the sand. "You have to admit some weird things have happened since you arrived."

It was time she stopped backing down. Otherwise she'd continue to live her life unseen and unheard. "Bookings canceled. Foaling alarms turned off. And now, a person who doesn't want to be identified has bought my land."

Zack released her shoulders and took a step back. "Maybe I'm dense. Explain to me why I'd want that land when all I want is to marry you and take you home."

"Let's be hypothetical. Someone is causing mischief. Not much, just small niggling things that make my business seem badly run. Small things designed to discourage me." She paused and took a deep breath. "Perhaps to discourage me enough to consider a fresh start, somewhere else."

There. She'd said it. Please, God, it wasn't true but since he wanted a heart-to-heart, she would tell him what was in hers.

Not all of it, though. If he knew she loved him, he would exploit that.

"You are accusing me of sabotaging your business to get you to marry me?"

It sounded preposterous when he said it. But secret

phone calls, secrets period. Closeting her here in the cottage, keeping her away from the stables... Skylar looked him full in the face, her heartbeat thumping loudly in her ears. Had she made a terrible, life-altering mistake?

Yet he hadn't denied it....

"Is a marriage to me so unappealing, you'd think I would resort to ruining you to get it?" he asked softly.

"Zack, tell me you think more of me than that. That it's not just the baby you want."

"What I think of you isn't the issue." He shook his head as if to clear away a fog.

"If you did those things because you cared for me, about me, then I could—I will—forgive them." She was that desperate.

"*If* I did them..." An icy light leapt to life in his eyes but the rest of him was still.

"If you didn't," she said urgently, "*tell* me you didn't, and I'll believe you."

Please tell me, she begged silently. There had to be some explanation for the strange events. One that didn't involve this honorable man standing in front of her now.

"I'm beginning to get the picture here." Zack pushed away from her and began pacing the small room. "I'm not good enough. Is that what you're saying?" He stopped and stared at her. "An uppity commoner from the bottom of the world who got lucky enough to plant his seed in the hallowed Fortune turf."

"That's ridiculous." That he could think that of her astounded her. Her birthright had nothing to do with who she was and no one had ever called her a snob before.

"No old money or tradition here," he continued, resuming his pacing. "Just a lowly businessman. Can't have any old genes cluttering up the family breeding ground."

Disappointment made her voice raw. "That's not it at all." She'd practically begged him to say he cared for her and his response was to throw snobbery in her face. He didn't get it.

Hadn't denied it, either.

"I thought we had a connection, something I haven't felt for anyone since Rhianne." He stopped again and ran his hands through his hair. "What a priceless joke."

Skylar shook her head. "I'm not laughing." She made for the door, tired and hungry. Angry and sad.

His clipped tones halted her at the door. "Maybe you're as shallow as your mother, after all."

She stopped but did not turn. "What's my mother got to do with this?" Skylar was getting a little tired of everyone dissing her mother. As far as she was concerned, that job should be reserved for her and Blake, no one else.

"Maybe all you want is the baby. Not the man. Not a relationship." He gave a hard sort of grimace that was probably meant to be a smile. "A baby accessory."

It was like a cold water slap in the face. He was a good shot. "You are so wrong, Zack."

"And you're totally wrong about me, too, Skylar. Ha!" There was no mirth in his exclamation. "So we do have something in common after all."

Skylar stalked across the room and snagged her still-damp jacket off the hook. "Not enough to base a marriage on." She opened the door. "I'm going to see my mother."

Eleven

Zack prowled the room like a caged animal. The cottage sat in the midst of a copse of trees, intensifying the roar of the wind. He peered blindly out into the night as rain lashed the windows. The minutes crawled by.

He should never have let her go. The cheap shot he'd fired about her being like her mother was purely a knee-jerk reaction to her accusations. Swallowing his anger, he knew how unwarranted it was.

He had only met Trina once but Skylar was nothing like her. In fact, he suspected she lived her life as the polar opposite of her mother. The dressing down, no interest in attracting men—save for one memorable occasion—her dislike of her mother's shallow pursuit of beauty, money and men, in that order.

And the biggie: there was no way in hell Skylar would ever abandon her child. Zack guessed that her mother's abandonment and her frequently mentioned disappointment at her daughter's choice of occupation left Skylar feeling unwanted and unloved. She would never inflict those feelings on her own child.

After an hour, he called her, spinning around when he heard her ring tone coming from the tote she'd tossed on the kitchen table. Zack swore viciously. They had a deal. It was one of his conditions that she be contactable at all times.

And she would have been if he hadn't upset her so much; she'd rushed out with only a thin jacket and her car keys.

Two hours after she'd left, he called her mother. The woman was subdued, saying Skylar had left an hour ago and, no, she hadn't mentioned going anywhere else.

That was a quick visit, he thought, calculating the distance from here to town. It was a thirty minute drive at the most, even in the terrible conditions.

The eaves of the cottage shuddered. He turned the evening news on, trying to distract himself from a growing worry. The local station reported on the storm, saying severe weather patterns were in play and already some of the streets of Sioux Falls were awash.

Zack called the big house and ascertained she wasn't there. With one eye on the TV, he then called Maya.

"She's left her phone here. Which way would she drive home from her mother's?"

Maya outlined a possible route just as the reporter on television said that wind had knocked all the traffic lights in the city out and there were widespread power cuts all over the region. As if to underline the point, the lights in the cottage flickered briefly.

"Is Creed home?" Maya asked.

"No." Zack got up, thinking he'd better find some candles. "Nash said he's staying in town because of the storm."

"I'll call him—you call Case and Gina."

Zack found Skylar's stash of candles and laid them on the table. Deeply worried, he put some water on to boil and then picked up the phone again.

Case and Gina were huddled up at their apartment in town. "Sioux Falls is notorious for flooding. She'd have to cross Skunk Creek, which sometimes flash floods."

Thanks for putting my mind at rest, Zack thought. "I'm going to take the truck and go looking."

"You stay there," Case insisted. "The streetlights are out in town and you're not familiar with the area."

Case promised to go looking and hung up, leaving Zack his cell phone number in case Skylar turned up. Maya called to say Creed was on his way to pick her up and they would scour the streets. Zack felt useless but she persuaded him that they were more familiar with the routes she was likely to go if required to detour. "Besides, when she turns up wondering what all the fuss is about, you can call us."

He saw the logic but it was excruciating to sit there by himself while his woman and baby were out in the storm with no means of communication.

As another hour crawled by and the storm intensified, his self-recriminations were bitter. He had reacted to her accusations by attacking her. He let his pride prevent him from saying what he wanted to say, what she needed to hear. That he loved her. That it wasn't just the baby he wanted. That she was the most precious and important thing in his life.

Why hadn't he told her? Pride and his fear she would shun him once she knew the truth about his dysfunctional family.

She wouldn't. Skylar couldn't have cared less. Deep down, he knew she was begging him to love her, even if she couldn't say it. But he'd let ego and righteous indignation get in the way.

Dammit! He would lose her if he didn't come clean.

A blast of thunder rocked the house and the lights flickered off for a few seconds. He moved to the window. The trees outside thrashed and swayed. The weather report said this was tornado weather, mild humid air, winds chopping and changing direction, heavy rain and now thunder. A couple of years ago this region was smashed by around fifty storms and tornadoes in a matter of days. The locals would not sleep tonight.

When he saw her next he wouldn't let her go. Ever.

That was, after he'd throttled her for going out without her phone.

After he'd come clean about his past and warned her of the scandal heading their way. The eagle-eyed reporters in this town who delighted in bagging the Fortunes at every opportunity would have a field day.

After he'd told her he loved her.

Skylar's chest pressed against the steering wheel as she leaned forward to peer through the windshield. The wipers were barely coping with the deluge.

Damn her mother. She eased a hand from its iron grip on the steering wheel and swiped at her cheeks. Damn pregnancy for turning her into a blubbering idiot. The fight with Trina had been spectacular.

After suffering the usual inspection—"Lovely cheekbones, darling. You get those from me. And your skin has improved with pregnancy…"—Skylar, still smarting from her fight with Zack, launched into her mother, demanding she swear she had nothing to do with Patricia leaving.

Stung, Trina denied it but then broke down in an uncharacteristic display of emotion and guilt. That's when Skylar discovered the ultimate betrayal.

Lightning flashed again, close, frightening her. It seemed like she'd been in the car for hours, fighting a growing panic. Why hadn't she gone to Maya's, or to the Fortune building or hotel? She imagined Zack's worry and anger at her for being without her phone.

That's if he was still there. After her disgusting accusations, he may well be on his way back to New Zealand. It was all so clear now. He may be overbearing and too protective at times, but manipulative? No way. Her stupid pregnancy hormones made her crazy. She wanted to hear that he loved her. He hadn't said that, but looking back, he had said he'd felt a connection, right from the start. Something he hadn't felt for another woman since Rhianne.

She wiped her eyes again and focused on that. He was still in his teens when he'd gotten Rhianne pregnant. That was a heck of a long time not to feel something for a woman.

Skylar's heart turned over. If that wasn't a declaration of love, it was pretty close to it. And he'd felt that when they met, not when he discovered the pregnancy.

Maybe everything wasn't about the baby after all.

But she'd gone and ruined it now, and all for nothing. Trina was the one responsible. The new stable hand, Ben, was her stooge, put there to cause trouble. He left Deme's stall unlatched and turned off the foaling alarms, as per Trina's instructions. She was responsible for the canceled mare and buying the land.

"I did it for your own good, darling," she'd pleaded. "You were wasting your life."

"Be honest, Mother. You did it to get back at Nash."

Skylar had long since accepted the shallowness and vanity of her mother. She only ever wanted anything to do with her children when doing so would strike at Nash. But to actively attempt to ruin her own daughter's business was unforgivable. "That's it. I want nothing to do with you ever again."

"You don't mean that." Trina's beauty-parlor-induced glow paled. "The baby…"

"I don't want my baby anywhere near your bitter poison."

She'd walked out with her head held high and a bruise on her heart. Whatever Trina's failings, she was still her mother. Now that Skylar was expecting, her own daughter cutting her off was something she could not imagine in a million years.

She shook off her pity. Her mother deserved no less. Because of her mischief, Skylar may have lost Zack for good.

Another mighty gust of wind rocked the car. The land agent had warned her about tornado weather. She peered into the blackness, aware that a twister would be on top of her before she'd see it. *Please, please get me home safely,* she prayed. *I need to tell him how sorry I am. I need to find the words to tell him that I love him.*

Finally, through the lightning and near-horizontal rain on her windshield, she saw the pillars of the estate up ahead. She'd made it.

Her relief faded when she pulled up to the cottage. The lights were out. He wasn't there.

She got out of the car and raced through a wall of water to her door, just as it opened. Skylar stopped with a jerk, peering through the murk at the broad shoulders crowding the doorway a foot in front of her. Her heart leapt with joy.

Short-lived joy. His hands gripped her shoulders and he shook her. "Dammit, are you *trying* to lose this baby?"

Skylar closed her eyes, too relieved to protest. Then his grip changed and he propelled her forward and into his arms.

"Thank God," he muttered, crushing her to his chest. Her arms were trapped and she couldn't hug him back. They stood on her porch, stinging rain whipping into every part of her, which meant he was getting soaked, too, but they stayed that way for long moments.

Finally he stepped back and pulled her inside.

Most of the storm noise was cut off abruptly when he closed the door. Zack led her to the fire and then left the room without a word. She stared around at the candles on the mantel and coffee tables. The power must have gone off, not unusual for a storm of this magnitude in these parts.

Zack returned with a couple of towels and a blanket. "Dry off," he ordered. While she mopped her face and hands, he pulled the sofa in front of the fire.

Skylar shook with cold and emotion but her most desperate need was the bathroom. Her bladder hadn't anticipated the long drive home. When she returned, mugs of steaming soup and a plate of sandwiches sat on the coffee table.

Zack picked up his phone. "Eat," he commanded, nodding at the snack.

"How did you…"

"I found a Thermos while I was hunting out candles." He punched some numbers into the phone. "I have everyone in the country out looking for you."

She wrapped her icy hands gratefully around a hot mug. Zack called Maya first, thanking her and Creed. Skylar hated that she'd worried everyone. Some people might find it gratifying that they'd caused such a fuss. Unaccustomed to attention, she just felt stupid.

Dialing again, he nudged the sandwiches closer, his eyes stern. She sighed, inhaling the steam off the cup of instant soup. Tomato. How did he always know just what she needed?

Zack finished talking to Case and stood looking at her. He looked more grim than angry.

Skylar gulped down a mouthful of soup and felt the too-hot liquid inch down her throat. "Those things I said earlier…" she stammered. "I just want to curl up and die."

He gave her an inscrutable look then sat down beside her and began unbraiding her plait. "What are you doing to me, woman?" His voice was gruff, his hands rough on her hair and she quickly put the soup mug down.

"Eat something, will you?" he said.

She picked up a sandwich and took a quick bite. Zack finished combing her wet hair out with his fingers and then picked up the towel and began rubbing her head briskly.

She sighed and put the sandwich down. "It was my mother." She closed her eyes while he rubbed her down like a horse. God knows what she looked like. "Ben's on her payroll. I hired him at her request. He's the son of a friend of hers. She paid him to cause trouble and she bought the land."

Zack ceased his rubbing and leaned back to peer into her face, his eyes questioning.

It hurt, saying it out loud. Her mother's complete disregard for her feelings astounded her—though she should be used to it by now. After all, this was the woman who had happily left her here with Nash when he kicked her out. Children were noisy, messy and a social no-no as far as Trina was concerned.

"To get back at my father mostly. I guess she thought hurting me, especially financially, would hurt him."

Zack stared at her. The last vestiges of anger drained away, and he looked more tired than she'd ever seen him, except for the long night at the hospital. Another night when he'd ministered to her, taken care of her, even though she'd brought it all on herself.

"I'm…sorry," he said simply.

Skylar shrugged again. "That's okay. I'm used to it."

"But you're her daughter, her own flesh and blood."

"So's Blake, yet she sold lies to the papers about him and Sasha breaking up." Zack nodded. "He told me."

"She's so bitter toward my father, she really doesn't think about anything except hurting him."

He stared at her face for a moment more and then tossed the towel down and laid a blanket around her shoulders. "You should get out of these wet clothes."

She pulled the blanket tightly around herself. "We won't have to worry about her anymore," she said heavily. "I've cut all ties, told her we're finished and that I don't want her to have anything to do with the baby."

Zack took her chin gently, bringing her face around to him. "Don't do that, Sky. You'll regret it."

His earnest tone surprised her.

"You can't turn your back on your parents, just like you and I will never turn our backs on little Amanda here." He swallowed. "No matter what she does."

She nodded, knowing it was the truth. "You're very forgiving after what I accused you of."

"I have to tell you something." He leaned back, his eyes serious. "It's going to come out any minute, anyway."

Skylar began to hope. Was he finally going to open up to her?

"My mother," he began, staring into the fire, "got pregnant at seventeen, with me. Her family was very wealthy, very powerful, politically. Back then, you couldn't get an abortion in New Zealand except on the street and they couldn't risk someone talking. So they had a family member fly her, against her will, to Australia for an abortion there."

Skylar closed her eyes in anguish. Not once, but twice. How could he bear it?

"But she got away, disappeared. I think she was genuinely afraid they would kill her, or me. She changed her name and never stopped running. I didn't find any of this out until after she died, but it fit. We never stayed in one place for more than a few months."

"Why didn't your father go?"

"They'd spirited her away in the middle of the night. He went to them, looking for her. There was an argument with one of her brothers, just a bit of pushing and shoving. The guy fell and hit his head but there were

witnesses present who said he was bashed from behind
with a poker as he left the room."

"There must have been evidence, fingerprints…"

"It was thirty-odd years ago. Forensics wasn't like it
is now." Zack shrugged. "Anyway, the family had the
police in their pockets."

"So he went to jail?"

"For quite a few years. When he got out, he had
nothing. I suppose he thought he may as well live up to
everyone's opinion of him. He spent most of his life in
and out of prison, petty stuff, mostly, until I found him."

Skylar tried to conceal her shock. How long had he
expected to keep it from her? "How do you get on with
him?"

Zack laid his head back on the edge of the sofa,
peering at the ceiling. "It's an uneasy relationship. It's
hard for him to trust. He's straight now, but he wants
his revenge and I can't blame him." He put his hands
behind his head. "Especially when the son of one of the
witnesses has backed Dad's story. A few months ago, I
bankrolled a court case against my mother's family so
he could have his day in court."

Skylar slid down off the sofa, still draped in the
blanket, and leaned against his legs. "What happened?"

"We lost. Politics is their game and they're good at
it. There have been two prime ministers in that family
and my uncle still heads the main opposition party.
There are elections coming up and it's entirely possible
that he could be our next prime minister."

"Have you met them?"

Zack shook his head. "I don't exist, just like my
mother ceased to exist for them when she ran away." He
looked down at her seriously. "The reason I've been

anxious to marry you so quickly is because my father has gone to the media. He tried it my way with the lawyers and it didn't work. The story broke over there last night."

"And your name is mentioned?" She frowned. "What *is* your real name?"

"My mother changed her name legally so I'm sticking with Manning. Her name was Greta Thorne. My dad is John Carter."

It was so much to take in. "Why didn't you tell me this, Zack? It would have explained so much."

He inhaled slowly. "I couldn't take the chance that you or your family would cut me out of the baby's life."

Oh, heck, of course he would think that. Her throat closed with sympathy and her eyes filled up again. "Just like your mother and then Rhianne," she whispered. "It's like history repeating."

"For the third time."

She rested her chin on his knee, not even caring that she was blubbering again. "Did you really think I would turn my back on you?"

He pursed his lips and let out a tense breath. "Not you, no. But I thought your father and brothers might. And if history *was* going to repeat, they would persuade you, or force you, into cutting me out."

A smile flickered across her lips and she shook her head. "They wouldn't succeed."

Zack dropped his hand, stroking her hair, and she slipped her arms around his leg.

"You would have me then?" he asked softly.

She sighed and rubbed her face against the still damp denims he wore. "In a Midwest minute."

Gently, he fisted his fingers and tugged her face up so she had to look at him. "What do you think your family is going to think of their Fortune princess hooking up with the son of a convicted murderer?"

"They'll back me, if I ask them to."

"It could get ugly," he warned. "Lots of headlines, especially once the papers here realize my connection to you."

"It'll be nice to be noticed for once," she told him with a wry smile. "I haven't exactly set the gossip pages alight with my nonexistent love life."

He gazed at her for a few intense moments. "I know I'm asking a lot, expecting you to give up everything and move halfway across the world. But I've been thinking. If you promoted Bob and I hired some extra help to run my businesses, we could split our living arrangements between here and New Zealand, depending on whose breeding season it is."

Skylar stared at him, overwhelmed. "I…don't know what to say." His concern and thoughtfulness reinforced her belief that Zack would make an exceptional father. She also realized that where they lived wasn't important, but the fact that he had offered the compromise was everything. "You don't know what it means to me that you said that," she told him haltingly. "Zack, I don't care where we live, as long as…" She closed her eyes, felt the old shy stammering Skylar Fortune flow back into her.

"It makes sense, Skylar. That way, Amanda gets to grow up with both her families."

"Both her grandpappies," Skylar agreed. "How does he, your father, feel about the baby?"

Zack looked thoughtful. "I'm hoping this will bring

us closer and also make up a bit for what he's missed out on all these years."

"I can't wait to meet him."

Zack leaned down and laced his fingers through hers. "It's taken me," he exhaled noisily, "eighteen years to find the woman I want to be with forever."

Her eyes brimmed and she ducked her head. Maybe if she wasn't looking at him, the constriction in her throat might ease a little. "Do you, Zack? Want to be with me forever?"

He squeezed her fingers. "If you don't know that by now, Skylar, then I don't know how else to show you."

His voice was warm but discussions about personal feelings crucified her. She was too shy to see if his dimples were showing.

"It's not just about the baby?" she mumbled into his knees.

"It didn't start with the baby—it started in January, when we met."

That was unexpected.

"There was something about you, even then, even before the night of the wedding," he continued. "Because you were so shy I didn't want to push it, but I'd already decided I was coming back in September. If I still felt the same zap, I *would* have pushed it, lady. Making love with you the night of the wedding just made me more determined." He tilted her head up so she had to look at him. "I kept in touch, remember? Every two weeks."

She wrenched her gaze away, staring into the fire. "I had this major-league crush but I sure as heck didn't know what to do about it."

"Until the wedding." Zack cleared his throat. "When I found out about the baby, well, I knew I couldn't lose this chance." He shook her fingers gently. "I haven't been celibate all these years, Skylar. But if I had gotten any one of those women pregnant, I'd have wanted to be involved with the baby but I sure as hell wouldn't have married them."

Her breath caught in her throat. Really?

"You were my special one," Zack murmured, "the one woman who made me want to consider forever."

Oh, she liked the sound of that very much. The baby rolled over. There was no other explanation for the fluttery exhilaration shivering through her. This was a lot to process and she had to respond but she was so lousy with words. "Zack, I…" She had to try. "You were the one for me, too. Only I never expected you to feel the same way. Things like this don't happen to me."

"Things like what?" he asked gently, stroking her hair.

She shrugged self-consciously. Someone get her a bag to put over her head. "You know. Feelings. Thinking about forever. Stuff like that."

He sighed. "Max reckons I'm good with the ladies but I'm sure making a mess of this." He lifted her hands off his knees and slid down until he was sitting on the floor beside her. "Look at me," he commanded, gripping her wrists tightly. "Help me out here. I'm in love with you, Skylar. Tell me you feel the same way."

Her eyes flew to his face and her mouth dropped open. He loved her, no, he was *in* love with her. "Oh," she said, wondering which was better. Love or in love.

They both sounded pretty darn good.

"Oh?" he asked, his brows almost meeting in the middle.

"I'm sorry, I'm not…" Her brain still wasn't functioning but her heart was rattling away at a gallop. She felt the smile start and was unable to stop it. And it got bigger and bigger, till her jaw ached and then Zack was smiling, too, right back at her. The two of them sat on the floor in front of the fire, holding hands and grinning at each other like idiots.

Finally, he shook his head and wiped his eyes. "Well, I'm not sure where that leaves us exactly but they do say a smile is worth a thousand words."

"I'm not very good at…" Her heart tripped again. She took a deep breath. "What *you* said. I love you, too." What a relief to finally get it out, even though her words *had* come out in a garbled rush.

Zack rubbed a hand over his eyes. "Perhaps you'll do better with a simple yes or no." He took one of her hands and brought it to his mouth, kissing each and every finger. "Skylar Fortune, will you marry me?"

Her heart was still jumping around like popcorn in the pan. The baby was squirming and the intense light in his eyes brought all the fine hairs on her neck and shoulders up. But at least her tongue seemed to escape from the knot it had tied itself into.

Skylar tugged his hand toward her and laid it on her cheek, still wearing that idiot grin on her face. "Yes, Zack Manning, I'd be honored."

* * * * *

Don't miss the final book in the
DAKOTA FORTUNES *saga.*
Be sure to pick up
FORTUNE'S FORBIDDEN WOMAN
by Heidi Betts, available this June.

Mediterranean Nights

Join the guests and crew of Alexandra's Dream,
*the newest luxury ship to set sail on the romantic
Mediterranean, as they experience the glamorous
world of cruising.*

*A new Harlequin continuity series
begins in June 2007 with
FROM RUSSIA, WITH LOVE
by Ingrid Weaver.*

*Marina Artamova books a cabin on the luxurious
cruise ship* Alexandra's Dream, *when she finds out
that her orphaned nephew and his adoptive father are
aboard. She's determined to be reunited with the
boy…but the romantic ambience of the ship and her
undeniable attraction to a man she considers her
enemy are about to interfere with her quest!*

Turn the page for a sneak preview!

Piraeus, Greece

"THERE SHE IS, Stefan. *Alexandra's Dream.*" David Anderson squatted beside his new son and pointed at the dark blue hull that towered above the pier. The cruise ship was a majestic sight, twelve decks high and as long as a city block. A circle of silver and gold stars, the logo of the Liberty cruise line, gleamed from the swept-back smokestack. Like some legendary sea creature born for the water, the ship emanated power from every sleek curve—even at rest it held the promise of motion. "That's going to be our home for the next ten days."

The child beside him remained silent, his cheeks working in and out as he sucked furiously on his thumb. Hair so blond it appeared white ruffled against his forehead in the harbor breeze. The baby-sweet scent unique to the very young mingled with the tang of the sea.

"Ship," David said. "Uh, *parakhod.*"

From beneath his bangs, Stefan looked at the *Alexandra's Dream.* Although he didn't release his thumb, the corners of his mouth tightened with the beginning of a smile.

David grinned. That was Stefan's first smile this afternoon, one of only two since they had left the orphanage yesterday. It was probably because of the boat—according to the orphanage staff, the boy loved boats, which was the main reason David had decided to book this cruise. Then again, there was a strong possibility the smile could have been a reaction to David's attempt at pocket-dictionary Russian. Whatever the cause, it was a good start.

The liaison from the adoption agency had claimed that Stefan had been taught some English, but David had yet to see evidence of it. David continued to speak, positive his son would understand his tone even if he couldn't grasp the words. "This is her maiden voyage. Her first trip, just like this is our first trip, and that makes it special." He motioned toward the stage that had been set up on the pier beneath the ship's bow. "That's why everyone's celebrating."

The ship's official christening ceremony had been held the day before and had been a closed affair, with only the cruise-line executives and VIP guests invited, but the stage hadn't yet been disassembled. Banners bearing the blue and white of the Greek flag of the ship's owner, as well as the Liberty circle of stars logo, draped the edges of the platform. In the center, a group of musicians and a dance troupe dressed in traditional white folk costumes performed for the benefit of the *Alexandra's Dream*'s first passengers. Their audience was in a festive mood, snapping their fingers in time to the music while the dancers twirled and wove through their steps.

David bobbed his head to the rhythm of the mandolins. They were playing a folk tune that seemed vaguely familiar, possibly from a movie he'd seen. He hummed a few notes. "Catchy melody, isn't it?"

Stefan turned his gaze on David. His eyes were a striking shade of blue, as cool and pale as a winter horizon and far too solemn for a child not yet five. Still, the smile that hovered at the corners of his mouth persisted. He moved his head with the music, mirroring David's motion.

David gave a silent cheer at the interaction. Hopefully, this cruise would provide countless opportunities for more. "Hey, good for you," he said. "Do you like the music?"

The child's eyes sparked. He withdrew his thumb with a pop. *"Moozika!"*

"Music. Right!" David held out his hand. "Come on, let's go closer so we can watch the dancers."

Stefan grasped David's hand quickly, as if he feared it would be withdrawn. In an instant his budding smile was replaced by a look close to panic.

Did he remember the car accident that had killed his parents? It would be a mercy if he didn't. As far as David knew, Stefan had never spoken of it to anyone. Whatever he had seen had made him run so far from the crash that the police hadn't found him until the next day. The event had traumatized him to the extent that he hadn't uttered a word until his fifth week at the orphanage. Even now he seldom talked.

David sat back on his heels and brushed the hair from Stefan's forehead. That solemn, too-old gaze locked with his and, for an instant, David felt as if he looked back in time at an image of himself thirty years ago.

He didn't need to speak the same language to understand exactly how this boy felt. He knew what it meant to be alone and powerless among strangers, trying to be brave and tough but wishing with every fiber of his being for a place to belong, to be safe and, most of all, for someone to love him….

He knew in his heart he would be a good parent to Stefan. It was why he had never considered halting the adoption process after Ellie had left him. He hadn't balked when he'd learned of the recent claim by Stefan's spinster aunt, either; the absentee relative had shown up too late for her case to be considered. The adoption was meant to be. He and this child already shared a bond that went deeper than paperwork or legalities.

A seagull screeched overhead, making Stefan start and press closer to David.

"That's my boy," David murmured. He swallowed hard, struck by the simple truth of what he had just said.

That's my *boy.*

"I CAN'T BE PATIENT, RUDOLPH. I'm not going to stand by and watch my nephew get ripped from his country and his roots to live on the other side of the world."

Rudolph hissed out a slow breath. "Marina, I don't like the sound of that. What are you planning?"

"I'm going to talk some sense into this American kidnapper."

"No. Absolutely not. No offence, but diplomacy is not your strong suit."

"Diplomacy be damned. Their ship's due to sail at five o'clock."

"Then you wouldn't have an opportunity to speak with him even if his lawyer agreed to a meeting."

"I'll have ten days of opportunities, Rudolph, since I plan to be on board that ship."

* * * * *

Follow Marina and David as they join forces to uncover the reason behind little Stefan's unusual silence and the secret behind the death of his parents....

Look for FROM RUSSIA, WITH LOVE by Ingrid Weaver in stores June 2007.

HARLEQUIN®

Mediterranean NIGHTS™

Tycoon Elias Stamos is launching his newest luxury cruise ship from his home port in Greece. But someone from his past is eager to expose old secrets and to see the Stamos empire crumble.

Mediterranean Nights
launches in June 2007 with...

FROM RUSSIA, WITH LOVE
by *Ingrid Weaver*

Join the guests and crew of *Alexandra's Dream* as they are drawn into a world of glamour, romance and intrigue in this new 12-book series.

HARLEQUIN

///// NASCAR

In February...

Collect all 4 debut novels in the Harlequin NASCAR series.

SPEED DATING
by *USA TODAY* bestselling author
Nancy Warren

THUNDERSTRUCK
by Roxanne St. Claire

HEARTS UNDER CAUTION
by Gina Wilkins

DANGER ZONE
by Debra Webb

On sale February 2007

And in May don't miss...

Gabby, a gutsy female NASCAR driver, can't believe her mother is harping at her again. How many times does she have to say it? She's not going to help run the family's corporation. She's not shopping for a husband of the right pedigree. And there's no way she's giving up racing!

SPEED BUMPS is one of four exciting Harlequin NASCAR books that will go on sale in May.

SEE COUPON INSIDE.

///// NASCAR

SPEED BUMPS
Ken Casper

She was born to race... deal with it!

www.GetYourHeartRacing.com   NASCARMAY

REQUEST YOUR FREE BOOKS!

2 FREE NOVELS PLUS 2 FREE GIFTS!

Silhouette®

Desire®

Passionate, Powerful, Provocative!

YES! Please send me 2 FREE Silhouette Desire® novels and my 2 FREE gifts. After receiving them, if I don't wish to receive any more books, I can return the shipping statement marked "cancel." If I don't cancel, I will receive 6 brand-new novels every month and be billed just $3.80 per book in the U.S., or $4.47 per book in Canada, plus 25¢ shipping and handling per book and applicable taxes, if any*. That's a savings of almost 15% off the cover price! I understand that accepting the 2 free books and gifts places me under no obligation to buy anything. I can always return a shipment and cancel at any time. Even if I never buy another book from Silhouette, the two free books and gifts are mine to keep forever.

225 SDN EEXJ 326 SDN EEXU

Name	(PLEASE PRINT)	
Address		Apt.
City	State/Prov.	Zip/Postal Code

Signature (if under 18, a parent or guardian must sign)

Mail to the Silhouette Reader Service™:
IN U.S.A.: P.O. Box 1867, Buffalo, NY 14240-1867
IN CANADA: P.O. Box 609, Fort Erie, Ontario L2A 5X3

Not valid to current Silhouette Desire subscribers.

Want to try two free books from another line?
Call 1-800-873-8635 or visit www.morefreebooks.com.

* Terms and prices subject to change without notice. NY residents add applicable sales tax. Canadian residents will be charged applicable provincial taxes and GST. This offer is limited to one order per household. All orders subject to approval. Credit or debit balances in a customer's account(s) may be offset by any other outstanding balance owed by or to the customer. Please allow 4 to 6 weeks for delivery.

Your Privacy: Silhouette is committed to protecting your privacy. Our Privacy Policy is available online at www.eHarlequin.com or upon request from the Reader Service. From time to time we make our lists of customers available to reputable firms who may have a product or service of interest to you. If you would prefer we not share your name and address, please check here. ☐

SDES07

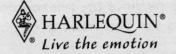

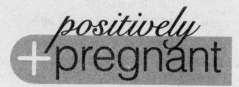

Silhouette Desire

COMING NEXT MONTH

#1801 FORTUNE'S FORBIDDEN WOMAN—Heidi Betts
Dakota Fortunes
Can he risk the family honor to fulfill an unrequited passion with the one woman he's forbidden to have?

#1802 SIX-MONTH MISTRESS—Katherine Garbera
The Mistresses
She was contracted to be his mistress in exchange for his help in getting her struggling business off the ground. Now he's come to collect his prize.

#1803 AN IMPROPER AFFAIR—Anna DePalo
Millionaire of the Month
This ruthless businessman is on the verge of extracting the ultimate revenge…until he falls for the woman who could jeopardize his entire plan.

#1804 THE MILLIONAIRE'S INDECENT PROPOSAL— Emilie Rose
Monte Carlo Affairs
When an attractive stranger offers her a million euros to become his mistress, will she prove his theory that everyone has a price?

#1805 BETWEEN THE CEO'S SHEETS—Charlene Sands
She'd been paid off to leave him. Now he wants revenge and will stop at nothing until he settles the score…and gets her back in his bed.

#1806 RICH MAN'S REVENGE—Tessa Radley
He'd marry his enemy's daughter and extract his long-denied revenge—but his new bride has her own plan for him.

SDCNM0507